About the Author

Photo: Peter Webber

Dermod Judge has been a designer, typographer, copywriter, dramatist, actor, broadcaster, international award-winning filmmaker, film and stage director, script writer and editor, international lecturer on storytelling and filmmaking. Now, having some time on his hands, he has turned to writing novels. His first, *Clash*, came out in 2017, the second, *Two Jam Jars For The Manor* came out the same year from the same publisher.

This novel involves dance and music, so, to enhance your enjoyment, there is a list of URLs (Universal Resource Locators) at the end of the book which will direct you to the webpage which features the great jazz classics and Irish folk songs referred to in the story. In an E book, the links can be clicked for direct access.

BOPPING IN BALLYMALLOY

Dermod Judge

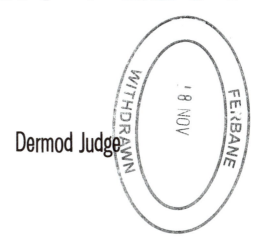

The Book Guild Ltd

First published in Great Britain in 2019 by
The Book Guild Ltd
9 Priory Business Park
Wistow Road, Kibworth
Leicestershire, LE8 0RX
Freephone: 0800 999 2982
www.bookguild.co.uk
Email: info@bookguild.co.uk
Twitter: @bookguild

Typeset in Minion Pro

Printed and bound in Great Britain by CPI Group (UK) Ltd, Croydon, CR0 4YY

ISBN 978 1912881 130

British Library Cataloguing in Publication Data.
A catalogue record for this book is available from the British Library.

To the many girls and women I danced with over the years.

1

The audition

He needed this part. He was thirty-five years of age and he knew that he was losing his edge as a dancer. Some of the other dancers at this audition were in their early twenties and fit as all hell. They could run rings around him but this wasn't the show for running. This show wasn't all about rhythm, although that was a prerequisite. It wasn't all about fancy moves, although that was what got the audiences to their feet. Nor was it about good looks. Hell! Some of those young men looked as if they still had their baby hair, and that didn't turn an audience at an expensive theatre on Broadway into adoring fans. This show called for an intelligent interpretation of the music and that was his speciality. If the most sophisticated audiences in America came to this show, they would want, demand, dancers who understood that this show was about the great American art form – jazz – at its most pivotal point, halfway through the American Century, and they would want lead dancers who knew that and could interpret the various types of jazz that would be played and the various dynamics – mostly racial – that would need to play out.

The announcements about the show, *Jazz*, excited him immensely. It sought to tell the story of the transition, after a successful and a just world war, of jazz from its traditional black roots through the white takeover with swing and its acknowledgment, even incorporation, of European conventions and musical structures and on to the subsequent reclamation by blacks through bop. All this against a revival of Dixieland. This was the period where superb and well-supported musicians had had to learn a second musical language – swing – to retain their fan base and their careers. Unfortunately, many of them were unable to learn a third language – bop or be-bop – and thus they faded from eminence. What this show required, apart from accomplished musicians to play the score, was lead dancers who knew the various musics involved. At this, he was good. His main strength was that he knew the music, having followed it passionately. He danced to enhance the music. To augment the intention that each type of music evoked. To get into and beyond the structure to the very core. To bring each note, solo, riff, phrase, chorus to physical life. To express with his body the emotion of the music and communicate his love for it. This was the show he had been waiting for and preparing for all his dancing career; and he knew he had, at most, three minutes to convince the producer and choreographer that this role was for him.

The auditioning dancers went through their routines and were dismissed with casual haste and a loud "Next!". Brutal as was the call to stop the music chosen by each dancer, he could only agree. None of the dancers had the sparkle, the sheer flair to separate themselves from the motley. Besides, their choices of music were appalling. Many had chosen pieces to which they had obviously been auditioning for years. Many were incongruent to the show's intention, and some pieces were so totally inappropriate that they were stopped after the first bar. After much soul-searching and deep, informed thought, he had chosen Stan Kenton's 1947 version of *The Peanut Vendor,* arranged by Kenton and Pete Rugolo, and had rehearsed to it with dedication, perseverance and love. He had an audacious plan – to tell the entire history of jazz in one routine. His opening, he believed, was the best he had ever done; a tense, barely perceptible swaying through the pounding guitar and tom-tom orchestral vamp at the start, to capture the Cuban magic then a more physical and jazzy movement of his lower limbs through the seductive trombone sequence that becomes brash and raw at the end of the chorus, at which he would break into a very sexy, all-body movement that really captured the swing era, leading into the discordance of bop when the trumpets and trombones battled for supremacy. Here, his dancing would become jerky and almost like a succession of freeze-frames. He was totally confident that the producers would see in this routine the entire structure of the *Jazz* show. He had the record in an envelope under his arm and nearly dropped it when his name was called. Down the aisle he walked, his heart pounding in spite of himself. On the stage, he handed the record to a person who stood next to a turntable and indicated the side he wanted played.

"Wait for my signal," he said and walked towards the front of the stage. He took a deep breath and strolled to the centre, snapping his fingers as he reached the spot. A faint crackle, the vamp started and he moved effortlessly into his routine. The trombone was halfway through the chorus when the word "Next!" echoed through the auditorium. Unbelieving, he staggered to a stop and the two figures in the second row came into focus. Their heads were close together as they conferred. He couldn't move. One of the heads turned towards him, and this time the shout was really loud.

"NEXT!"

He was a child of the streets and the beer halls and the music halls and the dance halls. The bawdy houses, the cold-water walk-ups, the post-war frenzy and freedom, the inter-ethnic tensions, the tough cops and the tougher women. All against the tatty backdrop of the restless tumult of mid-20th-century big-city

America. Most of all, he was a child of dance. Jazz dancing. He had studied jazz so that he could interpret it in dance and, as he studied, he looked for hooks; some clearly identifiable break, solo, riff, chorus or flavour, from wherever in the world it had come, that would inspire moves which would give additional meaning to the foot and body work he cultivated and was so proud of.

And there were, at least, plenty of flavours to choose from, brought to the great crucible of the deep American South, especially to *Noo Awlins*, as the hodgepodge of the city on the Mississippi River was called by its residents. In the 19th century, as America was shaping itself, many of them came from, or rather, were ripped from, Africa and the Caribbean and catapulted into slavery. The great commentator C.W. Cable sang them out 'like the roll call for the last trump'; Mandingoes, the merchants of Africa; Foulahs, of the rosy cheeks; Sosos, Popoes, Cotocolies, Agways, Nagoes and Fonds, light-skinned Ibos, ferocious Aradas and Yorubaasm, Malinbs and Ambrices.

And out of that slavery came jazz; the music of the oppressed. Born of the call-and-response work song of the fields, which was the slaves' way of offering comfort to the fellow oppressed in a form and language not to be understood by the oppressor, it soon moved to the dusty streets of the Southern cities and into the reeds, valves and bells of the adopted military musical instruments commandeered by the slaves as well as the keyboards of the whorehouses, the drinking dens and the dancehalls. It was as if the age-old slang or argot of the murky levels of society, where solid ground ends and ooze begins, was rendered in a music that grated on the sensibilities of the genteel slaveowners. Jazz, like slang, was a dark beast of the night. Ugly, discordant and tuneless to those who could not or would not listen. The burying songs of the oppressed epitomised this. They started with death marches and sombre swayings on the way to the cemetery but burst inescapably into such acceptance of human weakness as *Didn't He Ramble* on the way back to town.

4

This offended many people attuned to the restrained, contained and more dignified bereavement behaviour of polite society: "Vulgarity in the face of death," murmured the elite as they shuddered. "Entertain the dead, don't lecture them," said the oppressed as they threw themselves on the graves and wailed in a minor key. The elite strove to contain this raw, untutored sound, and when that didn't work, they absorbed it and thus thought they had beaten it. But jazz prevailed. The word, anyway, was a euphemism for the raw, single syllable, single-note word 'fuck'; as in *fuck slavery, fuck white society, fuck whitey*. And if that wasn't enough to frighten the horses, along came the blues; twelve bars of anguish, crude and vulgar, which was then, and is now, the true test for a jazz player or singer. Jazz changed as the century progressed; migrating negroes, sound recording and the phonograph brought the music to more people and more people to the music, which was and remained in a perpetual state of flux. With radio, the flood became a torrent of biblical proportions, worthy of a rousing verse in the spirituals. Folk ballads, ragtime, stride piano, ragged guitar pickers on locomotives, white-suited orchestras in opulent ballrooms all joined in, causing excitement, bewilderment and confusion in equal proportions. In a speakeasy on Rampart Street, Jelly Roll Morton claimed to have invented jazz on a Cunard voyage and when a black blues singer sang *My Daddy Rocks Me with One Steady Roll*, a New York matron, with tears in her eyes, cried, "My dear, my dear. How beautifully you sing negro spirituals."

One thing that cemented all these musical trends together was improvisation. It went against the established tradition of European music but, in reality, it harked back to the creative roots of every musical form embedded in every society in the world. Our child of the dance understood this and learned from it but his era, his time on the jazz timeline, hadn't come yet. It was ushered in by a group of young blacks, not from the deep South but from all over the States. In fact, they believed they had nothing in common with the Southern Negroes, by whom they were perceived as upper-crust. They were mostly from comfortable middle-class homes and were drawn to popular music and jazz because it sounded fun and because the classical music world was rigidly segregated. They mostly had conservatory training, so they had a lot to contribute to jazz when they confronted and joined it. They could create part-harmony with ease and that, specifically, was what jazz needed to break out of its rural cocoon. Eventually, they helped instil respect among musicians for pure musicianship and the ability to play difficult arrangements with skill. They were there when the equal *boom-boom, boom-boom* beat of *Noo Awlins* jazz changed into the unequal *boom-ta-ta, boom ta-ta*, of the cities. This emancipated rhythm took off and became a building block of swing. This was the era in which our child of the dance came into his own. Swing took over and ruled until nudged slightly aside by a revival of the 'Dixieland' clarinet, trumpet and trombone ensemble that again allowed simultaneous improvisation which swing had begun to lose the knack of or the desire for. Swing had fallen into the trap of sequences of flashy but unrelated solos, topped and tailed by equally unrelated riffs. But swing corrected itself and with the help of the airwaves, grew massively. Then, out of the blue, new forms, new improvisations, new rhythms and new names came on the scene, made by ferociously talented young black men, the most important of which was bop.

Bop was 'created' – a deliberately chosen word within the jazz world. It was not so much an evolution but a new way of making music created by an exclusively black group who were annoyed at the manner in which the white musicians had commandeered the heights and rewards of swing. To begin with, they moved from the swing tempo of 200 beats per minute up to above 300 beats, which few musicians could manage. To rub salt in the wounds, they played ballads as slow as 80 beats per minute, too slow to dance to. But even when playing this slow, the wily ones would cram in so many notes that they were, in effect, playing fast at a slow tempo. Tough work for a dancer. But our dance-child sought a way and found several. So, after the Second World War, when the shifting social forces in society were being echoed by changes in popular music and jazz, he was up among the most promising professional dancers in New York, where our story begins.

2

The car

The car was almost too wide for the Irish country roads. When he met a very occasional car coming the opposite way, he stopped on his side of the road and let the other pass him. With this technique, he had avoided scratching the glistening sides of his vehicle, but the passing cars were not often so lucky. The drivers were so distracted looking at his beautiful automobile that they drifted onto the soft verge and into the brambles that reached out from the thick hedges on either side. Strangely enough, not one of them had complained at his inordinate share of the road. It was as if being shouldered aside by such a car was more of a privilege than an inconvenience.

The frequent flocks of sheep and cattle were another thing altogether. They were invariably being flogged along at a fast walking pace by astoundingly ragged and ill-tempered drovers with long, crooked sticks in their hands and a plentiful supply of short brutal expletives in their mouths. He would stop in the centre of the road and put the handbrake on. The scurrying clumps of animals would divide in two, and the sheep would slide past oblivious and the cows with vacant interest. Neither so close that he worried for his paintwork, which indeed was in more danger from the drovers, whose focus on their bovine charges was so intense that, happening upon the car's hood unexpectedly, they came close to delivering a heavy blow on it with their sticks.

Why he, Curly Collins, was in Ireland at that particular time, in that car, a 1948 Buick Roadmaster with the famous waterfall grill in front of him, a wooden box of jazz and swing records on the seat behind him and a wind-up gramophone in the rear trunk, is worth recounting. After his humiliating rejection for the show *Jazz*, he had left New York, collected the Buick bequeathed to him by his recently deceased Uncle Michael and gone on an extended tour of America, just as the Interstate Highway was being planned but not yet built. So, he had to subject his Roadmaster to varying qualities of roads which, as it tipped the scales at around 2,000 kg, made some of the stretches a little hairy. Even though power steering had been installed in his model, the curves demanded some serious attention, but nothing to the attention required for the twisting Irish roads that lay ahead.

As he travelled, news of *Jazz* kept overtaking him as it played to capacity houses from its opening night. Instead of launching him into another stage of his dancing career, the rejection had damaged his standing in the dancing fraternity as well as his self-respect and reduced his career to occasional demonstrations at the clubs, and he even danced for a fee with some frustrated middle-aged women. But he never went home with them. That would have buried him. The reasons for his failure tormented him for a long time, but he finally figured it out. He had been good and had danced superbly, but so had the many other top level dancers who had auditioned. The problem was that he had danced essentially the same as all the rest. There had been no difference between any of them, and the first few moves he had made had signalled that fact to the producers. When this painful realisation had finally dawned on him, the show was off Broadway and touring Europe, so he never saw the final production, but he would bet his Buick that the dancer who had landed the part he had auditioned for would have been different, with a unique style. He had often thought long and hard about the giants of dance who had changed the industry forever and had often been imitated, seldom equalled and never excelled. There was Fred Astaire who could handle a hefty woman at any speed on any film set to any music with a deft elegance that tempted many a middle-aged man risk a hip joint with the wife. There was Gene Kelly, who could scale a wall as if he was doing a tango, and the Nicholas Brothers, whose leapfrogging into full ballet splits and rising again without bending their legs caused grown men to wince.

The reasons he found himself licking his wounds in Ireland were a little tortuous. His uncle had many a story about his times, and Curly had listened to them with deep interest; not that he believed them but they were such *grand* tales. After a few enjoyable weeks in the Dublin pubs, he decided to head for West Cork to the place where the much-lamented soldier and statesman, Michael Collins, died: *Beal na Bla*, the Mouth of Flowers. This was prompted more by his fond memories of his uncle and his bequest of the Buick, than actual interest in Irish politics.

All this was good for a pint or two shared with inquisitive Irishmen, attracted by his strangeness and his car. America was in good odour throughout the Western world in the 1950s. The yanks had won an undoubtedly just war. They were physically enormous, thanks to copious food and clean, bracing air. They had invented jazz, which was still seeping into the consciousness of many countries but still carried an exciting cachet. And the renowned technology of America was exemplified by the Buick, huge in its presence and dominance in traffic. He knew his fair share of Irish rebel songs and had what could be called a barroom baritone and so was welcome company wherever he went. So, he left Dublin with a hangover and the tune of many a folk song stuck in his mind. In the pubs, he had been surprised at the love the Irish had for their songs. Not for them, the frothy popular songs about love unrequited, love longed for, love rejected or unnoticed, or love everlasting. There were a few about love for Mother MaCree, for Ireland or for a woman who represented it, but the true Irish love songs were plaintive and aching, and many about the last visit or vision of a betrothed who died before the marriage. Those songs could still a pub full of inebriated Irishmen quicker than a visit by an after-hours policeman. Generally, though, they were rebel songs about the various uprisings through the long years of oppression, all of which up until the Easter Rising (of 1916) had inevitably been squashed by the English colonists, and the roll call of dead patriots was long and melodious. His favourite became *Down by the Glenside*, after he had heard it in pubs from the Phoenix Park to the outer reaches of Rathfarnham. Stuck in his head was the smooth tune and the powerful line:

'We may have good men but we'll never have better.'

In this was encapsulated the Irish penchant for brave heroes, safely dead.

Once out in the country on the narrow, rather winding roads, heading west, the road signs intrigued him. They too spoke of the history of Ireland represented by the names of places. They had the name in English in capital letters and the Irish name inscribed above in lower case. The first that caught his eye was Leixslip, and on the strength of it he decided to stay for the night. The name seemed a meaningless English word, but above it the Irish name was *Leim an Bhradain*. Even badly pronounced, it sounded more intriguing. He pronounced the name as 'Lem and Bradden' and even wrote it down in his notebook and then started to look for a place to stay for the night. He soon found a low-roofed hotel that looked comfortable, so he checked in and headed for the bar and the pint he had become so addicted to.

It was cosily warm, thanks to a glowing fire and the smile and bonhomie of the man behind the bar.

"Come in, come in. Warm yourself and have a drink. A warm skin and a cool throat, that's the divine right of humankind."

"A pint, please," said Curly, taking a seat at the bar facing the fire. "Nice place you've got here."

"Thanks. It's been in my family for five generations," said the barman, starting the pint.

"So, you're the owner?"

"Indeed, for my sins. But it's better than having a pub for your virtues."

"Yes, it sure is," replied Curly, not understanding the man's meaning. Another man came in, rubbing his hands and nodding his head benignly.

"Ah, here's the Doctor," said the barman as he started another pint. "The wisest man in Leixslip. Not that that's much to boast about. We're a dim lot here. Evening, Doctor. Just in time. Now this gentleman won't have to drink alone."

The Doctor was a rotund man in a houndstooth sport jacket at least two sizes too big for him. It hung on his frame like a damp horse blanket. There were six pens and pencils in his top pocket, a feather in his vaguely Alpine and battered hat and enormous stains on the legs of his trousers.

"Evening, Jim. That's good." He turned to Curly in a confidential manner. "Drinking alone is the curse of the Irish. Drinking alone gives you weak bowels and shaky legs. It splits families, divides communities and confuses the dogs. But drinking in company, good company, exalts us in honour and estimation." He held out his hand. "Jack Haggerty, but everybody calls me Doctor. Christ alone knows why."

"Curly Collins." Curly shook the hand.

"And I'm Jim," said the barman, "and there's your pint. The finest in Ireland."

"I'm sure it is," said Curly, taking the proffered pint.

"He's not kidding, you know," said the Doctor. Arthur Guinness had his first brewery here in Leixslip, before he moved to James's Gate in Dublin. Cheers."

Jim kept a reverent silence while the two attacked their pints. A moment to savour, to smack the lips and to replace the glasses on the bar, the exact half-inch of creamy froth showing no impression of their lips.

"It's like going back on the breast," said the Doctor. "Is that your chariot out there?"

"It is. It's a—"

"Buick Roadmaster. 1950?"

"1949."

"Is it, bejaysus? Can you manage the roads around here?"

"It's a bit tight on the sharp corners."

"I'm sure it is." The doctor settled his elbow well and truly on the bar and slumped into a comfortable position, ready for good chat, while Jim rested both elbows on his side of the bar.

"What brings you to this place?"

"My uncle, Michael Collins."

They both straightened up at the name.

"Not the Big Fella," said Curly. "His cousin. He left Ireland after Collins was shot. He was disgusted with the way things were going here."

"As well he might be. Collins should have been our first president, instead of the long hoor."

"De Valera?"

"The same. However, it's too early in the evening to go back there. Are you away to *Beal na Bla?*"

"The Mouth of Flowers. I am. My uncle would have approved of me going there."

"I'm sure he would." The Doctor took another healthy mouthful and the froth remained pristine. "Half the women of Ireland were in love with Michael Collins."

"He was a grand sight," Jim butted in. "Strutting around

13

Dublin with a price on his head, in full view of the English and their minions. And they never saw him."

"It proves that you hide in full sight if you're cocky enough," said the Doctor.

"At the same time, the Dubliners were saying, 'There goes the man. Isn't he grand?'"

"And the English were saying, 'It couldn't be him! He wouldn't dare!'"

The two savoured the memory, the one sipping and the other looking at his enjoyment with satisfaction.

"Where did you get the name *Curly*?" asked the Doctor. "Your hair is a straight as the road to Hades."

"It's short for Cornelius," replied Curly, knowing he was feeding the Doctor.

"Cornelius? That's a name you don't hear much of nowadays," said the Doctor, glad to have a verbal launching pad. "It's a translation of the Irish name Conchubhar – Connor in our current mealy-minded language. By Christ, the old Irish could spell! And we have had many such since. If I'm not mistaken…" He turned to Jim who shook his head at such an impossible concept. "… Connor means dog lover."

The Doctor contemplated his pint for a while before continuing, leaving Jim in a state of suspended amusement and Curly in a similar mood.

"But…" continued the Doctor, having milked the suspense with the unerring instinct of the Irish story spinner, "… you're of Irish distraction, as they say. I'm wondering how you had that name inflicted on you."

Curly was intent on furthering the conversation. "I had an aunt who said that it was the name of a Roman who was told by an angel to seek Peter."

"And where did that tall tale come from?" asked the Doctor.

"From the New Testament," replied Curly, hoping to see the Doctor flummoxed.

"That mishmash!" the Doctor expostulated. "Sure, wasn't it written by four men who contradicted each other, every chance they had?" Jim looked nervous and Curly looked expectant. "We're a sceptical lot, the Irish. We take all stories with a grain of salt. Even those told by Matthew, Mark, Luke and… what's his name…?"

"John," said Jim, surreptitiously crossing himself behind the bar at such blasphemy. Curly was amused at the lengths an Irish pub raconteur would go to for effect. He took a leisurely drink and then took a notebook out of his pocket.

"By the way, I'm interested in the road signs and the way they show the names in two languages. In Irish, this place is… Lem and Bradden?"

Jim and the doctor both smiled.

"Not bad for a yank. *Leim an Bhradain*. It's an interesting name, Leixslip," said the Doctor, sticking his two thumbs into his waistcoat pockets and straightening in full declamatory manner, and Jim settled down for what was obviously another display of the town's erudition. "It's an adaptation of the Old Norse name *Lax Hlaup*. If I'm pronouncing it properly, it's merely a slip of the tongue." He waited for acknowledgement of his verbal dexterity and Jim obliged:

"Leixslip! A slip of the tongue!" he said. "That's a rare one, even for you, Doctor."

The Doctor nodded modestly and continued.

"It means Salmon Leap, which is *Leim an Bhradain* in Gaelic. So, the history goes round and round. They all left their marks on the place names here; the Vikings – Norwegians as well as Danish – the English, and of course, ourselves. You're right to look at the road signs. Most of the places were renamed by the English who anglicised the Irish names and took away some of the reasons for the names. Mullingar in Irish was *Muileann gCarr*, the left-handed mill. Who knows what that meant? But my favourite is Ennistymon, way out west in County Clare. In

Irish, it's *Inis Dioman*, the Isle of the Devil. Christ alone knows why. Other Irish names mean the 'Plain of Stone', that's *Maghnala* or Mallow. Then there's the 'Hill of the Virgin'. That's *An Cnoc*, Knock, where Mary appeared. There's Ballinnasloe, *Beal atha na slua,* which comes from 'Moat at the Ford of the Crowds'. Place names are great fun. They tell you things you should know. But you have the same thing in America. All over the place."

Curly was taken by this thought. "I suppose we do. We've got, let's see, Seattle, who was an Indian chief; Utah, the name of an Indian tribe."

He thought a bit and they kept silent. "There's Indiana, but I suppose that's an English name. Still... there's Colorado, that's Spanish for red. There's Arkansas... and many more I can't think of just now. I never thought of it that way."

"You see, Curly, it's the same all over the world," said the Doctor. "The various people leave their marks on the land just like the glaciers did as they scraped their way along. The later peoples who came along tried to wipe the map of the previous dwellers and impose their own destiny. But the first names almost always told more about the place named. There! That's the end of the history lesson. Another pint there, Jim. My belly thinks my throat is cut."

The talk and the badinage increased in direct proportion to the amount of Guinness consumed, and the Doctor was great value through it all. Some snacks of prawns and cheese and pickled onions and heavily buttered soda bread were produced and disposed of. Generally, Liexslip also gave great value and, when they called it a day, the two locals and the guest were satisfied, the former for having acquitted themselves well in the town's entertainment of strangers and the latter for having kept up the reputation of the United States of America and of a returned Irishman to the land of his begetting. So Curly went to bed in a comfortable state of intoxication and the next morning continued on his journey.

3

The ascendancy

He'd been interested in horses since his boyhood and could ride pretty well, so he headed south to see the Curragh, the renowned horse breeding and racing plain in Kildare, hoping that he could arrange a horse for a few hours. He stopped to fill up the Buick in the town of Kildare and was answering the usual questions about the car from the petrol attendant when a dusty old Rolls Royce pulled in behind him and a tall man in tweeds got out. He was looking at the car with interest and Curly knew that he was in for another grilling, but he decided that this was the sort of man who could arrange a horse for him, so he smiled widely as the man approached, with his hand outstretched.

"Good morning. George Rathbone's the name. I live around here."

"Curly Collins. I'm taking a tour of Ireland right now," said Curly, taking the hand.

"And here to see the Curragh?"

"Yes, in fact. How did you guess?'

"You have the look of a riding man about you. Excuse me. Fill her up, please, Joe."

"Certainly, Mr Rathbone," said Joe, taking the key and scurrying to the Rolls.

"And the usual checks. Oil and things." He turned back to Curly. "I say, do you mind if I have a look at your car?"

"Not at all. Take a ride in her," Curly replied, offering the keys.

"I say, that's confoundedly kind of you, Collins." He grabbed the keys and got into the driving seat. "Back in a few minutes, Joe."

"No rush, Mr Rathbone. I'll drive the Rolls home, shall I?"

"That would be very kind of you."

Rathbone approached the Buick and surveyed it.

"A Roadmaster, I believe. What year?"

"1948. Straight eight, four-barrel carburettor, 170 horsepower."

"I wonder if we are meant to go as fast as that could take us."

"One trip and you'll be convinced that we are. It feels so good it can't be wrong."

"Sinners have been saying that ever since we invented sin. What on earth are those holes?"

He meant the three Ventiports on the swooping fenders.

"Well, the designer liked airplanes and that's how he showed it, from a fighter plane design. He even put flashing lights inside them."

"My word!"

"But they closed them up on later models. A pity."

Rathbone turned on the engine and put it into drive. The car whispered forward smoothly.

"I know where I can open it up and put it through its paces. On the road through the Curragh. Okay?"

"Okay. You're driving."

Rathbone enjoyed himself for the next half hour, and Curly enjoyed seeing his pleasure, especially when it went around a tight turn and kept a very straight line when it came out. Finally, Rathbone stopped and switched off the engine. They listened to the wind in the trees and the faint birdsong for a while and then he spoke.

"Come to the house for lunch."

A few minutes later, they drove through tall ornamental gates slung from massive stone pillars with 'Rathbone Hall' engraved on them. They pulled up on the sweeping gravel road which led up to a substantial double story house surrounded by some rather small oak trees.

"The original trees were burnt down a few years ago. I'll never see these ones in their full growth, I'm afraid."

Inside the house, he was directed to a small washroom to one side of the hall where he freshened up, and when he emerged, he was ushered into a sunny room at the back of the house. A moderately sized table was laid for lunch and Rathbone was seated at the head. He gestured towards a chair at the far end where Curly took his seat.

"I dine alone most time nowadays, so I'm always on the lookout for strangers to liven up the lunch table. Some Chablis?"

"Thank you."

A butler materialised out of nowhere and filled his glass with white wine and then efficiently served a modest lunch of fish and salad.

"So, what do you make of this country of ours, Collins? Don't hold back. I love Ireland, mainly because there are conflicting views about everything, particularly its history."

"I was – am – amazed at how history dominates almost every social gathering I've attended."

"Yes. There is rather a lot of history for such a small country. America, now, is vast. History can get lost there in those wide-open spaces and far-apart cities. Here we live cheek by jowl. Consider the Rathbone family. We are of what used to be called, and is still considered by some, the ascendancy – Protestants who are used to addressing the native Irish from horseback. This piece of land was given to our family by the Crown in the 14th century, and I inherited it from a man who epitomised the cleavage line between Irish Catholic and English – or Anglo-English Protestant.

The blood in my body is, in fact, a somewhat explosive blend of both factions. You seem interested."

"I'm fascinated. Michael Collins was an uncle of mine. And my family speak of him with great respect."

"Well deserved, I assure you. Every woman in Ireland was in love with him. Well, you shall hear the Rathbone epic, but it is more suited to the after-dinner hour. You'll stay, I hope, and I have more than enough room to accommodate you for the night."

Curly tried to demur but he was politely but firmly persuaded.

"Good. And now a relaxed overview of the estate from horseback would seem in order. You ride, I assume. All Americans are cowboys at heart."

***

An hour later, Curly and Rathbone were each mounted on a superb horse, reared and trained on the Curragh, an extensive grass-covered, well-drained ridge of sand and gravel on a sedimentary layer of limestone; the perfect ground for such activities. Rathbone noticed, with approval, Curly's confident and secure seat on the huge bay mare as they cantered leisurely up to the first viewing site, where they stopped and surveyed the countryside up to and beyond the tall crenelated wall that defined the extent of the estate.

"My great-grandfather built that wall, to give the locals something to do – for which they got paid, I hasten to say. I hate it. I'd have preferred a ha-ha."

"What on earth is a ha-ha?" said Curly, laughing.

"A wall that's recessed into the ground on the inner side of a declivity. It forms a serious barrier but it doesn't obstruct the view. That... thing! Offends me."

Rathbone put his spurs to his horse and they continued on the inspection of the estate, of which he was obviously very proud.

"You still... own the land?"

"Oh yes. We Anglo-Irish are a canny lot. When independence came and things started to normalise, we ducked our heads down, and when the dust had settled and we had different rulers, we still owned vast tracts of land, some towns and villages, the breweries and distilleries and many of the major commercial ventures. As the French say; *plus ça change, plus c'est la même chose* – the more things change, the more they stay the same. We are nothing if not resilient. Can you manage that gate?"

Curly put the bay at the four-bar gate and sailed over it with ease.

***

After a warm bath, a change of clothes and a substantial supper washed down with two fine wines and a vintage port, the two of them were seated in comfortable armchairs in Rathbone's study, the brandy was on a low table between them and a fire was glowing soothingly in the grate.

"And now, the Rathbone epic?" Curly asked.

Rathbone settled himself and looked into the fire while he collected his thoughts.

"My father, James Rathbone, considered himself mostly Irish and was very concerned for the country. In spite of that, the class divisions here and in England were amongst the most extreme in the world. It was possible for people who lived in close proximity to each other to lead parallel lives; in fact, many of the natives of Ireland were invisible to the ruling class, of which my father was so proud. There was, however, one exception..."

***

"Pat Tierney was a groom at Rathbone Hall and, for most of his youth, enjoyed his life there. He was playmate to my father and shared, as much as it was possible, in his lifestyle. The fact that he was the groom helped because the local gentry were besotted with horses. He was also allowed to attend the fox-hunting excursions that were held regularly, and the members of the hunt frequently consulted Pat on the problems they were having with their horses. James Rathbone basked in the limelight that Pat's skills created and tried to accrue some acknowledgement for the advice offered. Pat didn't mind and the locals were prepared to indulge this pretence by a member of a powerful family. Pat was a superb horseman and helped keep the ten horses in the stables fit and in fine condition, but his unashamed favourite was a big black stallion called, appropriately, Lucifer, and he was the only person that could control the beast. Others tried but were suffered so reluctantly on his back that they spent the time riding in a state of extreme nervousness, which Lucifer sensed. So, he tried to discomfort them further with a series of antics that brought home, forcibly, to each rider, just how far he (no woman dared get on his back) was from the ground on a fifteen-hands-high brute with no respect for humans. Riding next to thorn bushes, darting under low hanging branches and brushing past the rough stones of a farm wall were some of the tricks the vindictive animal tried with them all. With the exception of Tierney. With him on his back, Lucifer behaved like the white Pegasus himself, soaring over obstacles, devouring the miles, exulting in the sheer physicality of horsedom.

"This, however, was a bone of contention with James Rathbone, the proud scion of the family and erstwhile playmate of Tierney. Lucifer was *his* horse, given to him by his grandfather, yet here he was, giving Tierney, a mere servant, the obedience owed to himself. He tried very hard to woo the horse away from Tierney, but nothing draws out the inherent qualities of a human like a dog or a horse; ready to give their fealty and obedience to those who deserve them, they instinctively seek out people who are equally ready to give their love in exchange. They will obey the others but reluctantly and submit to their instructions in a surly manner. Not for them would they break their bones and burst their hearts; and no amount of abuse or anger will extract that ultimate gift – the glory and joy of complete trust between man and beast. So, James Rathbone 'mastered' Lucifer through the liberal use of spur, whip and bit as well as copious sprays of swear words. The horse submitted but with such bad grace that riding him became an unpleasant experience; and James compensated for the loss of his recalcitrant horse by riding a big, powerful but docile bay, secretly hoping that Lucifer would notice the snub, but the black stallion didn't seem to mind. This was the beginning of the gradual estrangement of the two youths.

"When the First World War started, the family head, Frederick Rathbone, had died, and James took over the house and its social duties. He was now in his late teens and had all the social graces of the ascendency, so he invited several local dignitaries to supper and held forth over the port.

'What's this I hear about a mutiny at the camp?' he asked of Lieut-Col. Stockwell.

'There's no mutiny at the Curragh,' replied Stockwell with asperity. 'Some officers have refused to disarm Carson's Ulster Volunteers, that's all.'

'But it was a direct executive order. That's mutiny as I understand it,' said a local bishop.

'Well, perhaps. But I cannot see the Crown taking sides against them,' said Stockwell, sinking his nose into his glass of port.

'Especially since the Irish have formed the Irish Volunteers to confront the Ulster Volunteers. Another typical Irish complication,' said a guest who had remained silent until then.

'But,' pronounced Stockwell, slamming his empty glass onto the table, 'his Majesty's Government...' At the mention of this august force, silence descended. 'His Majesty's Government...' Stockwell continued... 'has actually offered Home Rule to these... Irish... these Irish Volunteers if they join the British Army *en masse*. Pass the port, please.'

'The political situation here gives me a headache,' said Rathbone. 'Let's talk about something less abstruse.' He had their attention. 'What are we, the non-military men around this table, going to do about the war?'

"The military men looked into the middle distance and remained silent, and the rest looked into their port glasses.

'Those of us who are of a fighting age will, of course, volunteer; but I am considering a more valuable contribution.'

"Most present joined the military men in looking into the middle distance, thinking this was going to be another appeal for money. But Rathbone caught them off guard.

'Not our money,' he said and they relaxed. 'I mean our horses...'

4

The legacy

"When James took over the Rathbone estate and affairs, Pat left his employ. None of the boyhood affection survived and, besides, Pat had become sick and tired of everything English, so he slipped into Dublin, joined the Irish Volunteers and attended the frequent illegal meetings at which the prominent Irish revolutionaries addressed the audiences and raised the patriotism of the Irish to a rabid state. During the day, he had a job on the Dublin docks, shovelling coal into the bowels of the ships that transported the Anglo-Irish families and soldiers to and from England, and the work stoked his hatred for the 'parasites' who embarked and disembarked. The work made him invisible to the authorities and he was left in peace for several months, but he was halfway through a six-hour shift of hard shovelling when the foreman appeared.

'Tierney!' he called.

'Yes. I'm here.'

"The foreman looked into the sky above Pat's head and had the grace to blush.

'I'm down here.'

'I know, Pat. I know. The boss has heard that the police are looking for you because of… well… because. So, he has to let you go. Right now. He suspects they'll be waiting for you at the end of the shift. They know everything, the fuckers.'

'And who tells them everything?' asked one of the workers. 'Answer me that.'

'Who knows? There's spies everywhere,' the foreman answered as he handed Pat a roll of paper. 'There's your money until the end of the week. Now go, while it's busy up there on deck.'

"Pat took the money.

'Tell him thanks. See you fellows.'

"He slipped off to a soft chorus of 'good luck' from his co-workers and headed up to the deck. Up there, it was as busy as the foreman had warned. A herd of horses were being loaded onto the deck in wide canvas slings suspended from a winch. He pulled his cap low over his face and scurried down the gangplank, passing the gang boss who winked at him as he passed. On the hard, he was about to slip away amongst the piles of crates and bundles when a scream drew his attention overhead. There, kicking and screaming in a canvas sling, was the unmistakable Lucifer who was in grave danger of slipping out of the restraint and crashing to the stones below.

'Lower the sling! For Christ's sake!' rang out from the deck in a voice he immediately recognised.

"There stood James in an army officer's uniform, his face red and his clenched fists raised over his head. 'That horse is worth a hundred of you lousy labourers. Be careful. Lower him. Slowly! SLOWLY!'

"Down came the sling in the nick of time; out of the sling came a thousand pounds of equine rage as Lucifer found his feet and started to gallop along the dock. Two armed soldiers, attracted by the commotion, came onto the hard as the horse galloped past them. Unslinging their rifles, they ran after it, closely followed by Pat. Lucifer ran into a veritable cul-de-sac of enormous crates and skidded to a halt at the end, turning to face the accursed humans. One of the soldiers raised his rifle to his shoulder but dropped it and fell to the ground as Pat cannoned into him and ran past towards the demented horse. He slowed to a stop a few feet from Lucifer and stood silently while the stallion looked at him, breathing heavily through distended nostrils and stomping his hooves on the ground. For a long minute, the two stood looking at each other. Then Pat stretched out his hand, slowly, and took a pace forward. The reaction was instant and threatening. Pat stopped and spoke carefully in a low, soothing tone.

'Lucifer. Lucifer. It's me. Your friend. Don't be afraid. Nobody wants to hurt you.'

"Murmuring softly, Pat approached the horse and, leaning his head inwards, laid it on the horse's and breathed in the exhalations from its nostrils. He then lifted both hands and laid them on the horse's neck, stroking it softly, murmuring all the time. Lucifer took some time but he calmed down and allowed Pat to take the dangling reins and start to lead him back to the ship. James was standing there and he was furious, but Pat put his finger on his lips and led the horse past him to where the sling lay on the ground. James followed to see how Pat would handle this and got a lesson on horse handling. Leading Lucifer forward, Pat positioned him over the sling which was stretched out flat so that the canvas now lay under the horse's belly. Pat turned back to James and indicated the long scarf he was wearing, with an unwrapping movement. James took the scarf off and handed it to Pat who, still murmuring, wrapped it gently over the horse's eyes, passed it under the neck and around to the back where he tied it. Then he nodded at James who, with the help of a sensitive stevedore, raised the sling gently and buckled it on the horse's back. The horse neighed nervously a few times but Pat's murmuring calmed him down. Then Pat caught the eye of the winch operator, who raised the horse gently off the ground.

Lucifer went up like a lamb, and Pat and James scrambled up the gangway and were there to unloose the horse and lead it to stalls that had been prepared. When Lucifer was settled in and peaceful, they both went back on deck.

'Shit!' said Pat, as he caught sight of four policemen who were marching along the dock, heading for the ship which Pat had been working on.

'They after you?' asked James.

'Yes. I've been betrayed.'

'Follow me.' James turned into the main structure on the deck, speaking over his shoulder in a low tone. 'You're my batman and groom and you're going to France. Any problems with that?'

'I'm not enlisted.'

'You soon will be.'

***

"So, the three of them went to war; the aristocrat, the rebel and the stallion and, miraculously, all three survived. The rest of the magnificent horses, of course, were slaughtered by machine guns in the first few days. Lucifer was so difficult to control amongst all the din and confusion that he was invariably left behind the lines when the rest were taken on patrol. Pat, perhaps, could have ridden him, but the social structure of the British Army forbade an enlisted man – which he was made in short order – to ride with troopers or officers. Pat and James were both smitten twice, by German bullets and by a gorgeous red-haired Irish *coleen*. The first in no-man's-land and the second in the field hospital where the redhead nurse soothed and comforted them after they were wounded. By the time they were sent home, they were both madly in love and insanely jealous of each other. Some more Cognac?"

Curly had been so enthralled by the narrative that he had to walk around to loosen up as George freshened their drinks and stirred up the fire. When they were settled again, George looked at Curly's expectant face and laughed gently.

"And now we jump forward to the end of this strange story. Don't look so disappointed, Collins. I said there was too much history in this country and, after all, we are only talking here about three people and a horse. They all came back. My father had married the redhead and Pat and Lucifer were back in the stables. You see, he had saved my father's life by carrying him back, badly wounded from no-man's-land after another futile attack, while he himself had a bullet in his stomach, quietly worming its way towards more vulnerable organs. So, my father was obligated to him, in spite of his boyhood resentments and Pat's love for my father's red-headed wife who, as a nurse in the field hospital, had healed them both of their wounds, despair and disappointment in life. So do obligations to other people entangle our lives.

"When they came back to Ireland, the war was over; the Easter Rising of 1916, forever sacred to the emerging nation, had happened, the few great houses remaining intact. This house was to be burned down shortly after the curtains had come down on our protagonists. But I anticipate myself. It was a fraught household. My father had grown to hate Pat, but my mother insisted on him remaining as part of the household. Pat was also burning with hatred but was tied down by those red tresses. It was a scandal in the neighbourhood; two men and a lovely woman cohabiting, so the place was out of bounds to the locals and to the few remaining members of the erstwhile ascendency.

"One afternoon, the two men had had too much to drink – again. The old butler, who moved around like a wraith, overheard the two of them in their cups and afterwards told my mother all that had transpired. She, of course, was horrified and took to her bed where she subsequently slowly languished and died, leaving me, the last of the Rathbones, to rattle around in this house which I had to mortgage to the hilt to renovate it after the Republicans

29

burned it down. So, the ignominious end of a historic family will sputter away with me. But it had its last macabre but bright blaze before it collapsed into embers.

***

'Why the fuck did you save me in France!' James bellowed.

'I wish I knew. I've regretted it ever since.'

'Regretted it? You have lived here like a lord's bastard ever since. Sponging off me.'

'And paying for it in humiliation!'

'I'm the one that's being humiliated. You have… estranged my wife. She's… besotted with you. The one valuable thing I have is my horse, and it's barely ridable since we got back. It can't go on.'

'And what do you intend to do about it?'

'Settle it, once and for all.'

'There's nothing I would like more.'

'Riding to hounds has always comforted me. Made me feel part of a superior, even noble society which you and the rest of the Irish rabble have dragged down and spat upon.'

'You have no hounds.'

'Unfortunately, that's true. But for what I have in mind, hounds are not needed. I want to stage a final hunt before the curtain falls on my people. I shall be the hunter and you the quarry. I shall ride Lucifer, the brute, and you shall be on foot.'

'You're mad!'

'Yes. I am mad. At you. At my wife. And at Lucifer. I want you all in hell, but since I cannot do that, I will do the next best thing. When I catch you, which I will, you will leave this place and this country, for ever. I will kill Lucifer and try to find some peace with my errant wife. Are you man enough for that?'

"Pat, who had been tortured by the time spent in the house, in the vicinity of the woman he loved and the horse that gave him a sense of his manhood, saw this as a way of ending his torture.

'I'll do it,' he said. 'If you catch me, I'll leave. But what if you don't catch me? What are the rules?'

'I've worked it out. We start at the sound of the seven o'clock church bell in the village, and we end at the sound of the eight o'clock bell. That is unless I overtake you and hit you with my whip, in which case I win. I will give you a five-minute start. There will be moonlight this evening and a clear sky. You must wear a yellow sash, so I have a chance of seeing you. The rest of your garments may be dark. You will have no trouble hearing or seeing me. Lucifer is sure-footed but never completely silent. If you make it back to the front porch before the bell, you win, and I'll give you Lucifer and one hundred pounds to disappear. During the hunt, you stay inside the estate wall and out of thorn cover.'

'I can go into a copse?'

'Yes, but you must not skulk. You must undertake, on your… honour (ha!)… to keep moving. Is that agreed?'

'Yes. And my honour is as important to me as to you. You've been thinking of this for a long time, haven't you?'

'Oh yes.'

"James looked at the clock.

'We have ten minutes before the bell. I will prepare Lucifer and you can prepare your garments.'

"The eavesdropping butler decided to tell my Mother about the grotesque hunt, but she had left strict instructions not to be disturbed, so the butler had to wait for her to summon her maid. He waited for a long time.

"When he had finished preparing the horse, James rode up to the front porch on Lucifer who whinnied to see Pat there. The scarf gleamed brightly in the light of a half-moon, reassuring James who dragged Lucifer's head away to the side so he could not see Pat. He pulled out his hunter watch and waited until the bell tolled the hour.

'You have five minutes start,' he said.

31

"Pat moved to the edge of the gravel. The sash remained in sight for a few moments and then abruptly disappeared. Knowing his prey, James also knew that he would stick to the rules, so he pondered about the direction he had taken. The surrounding, widely spaced trees offered no effective cover for a human, so he must have moved in behind the clump of low laurel bushes. Now he knew at least his initial direction. Thinking hard, he drew up in his mind the features of the estate they had both grown up in and explored in depth. He conjured in his mind the declivities, the sunken paths, the many rivulets that flowed through the landscape and the thickets that were scattered about and through which he – and Pat – had scrambled in their youth.

"When the five minutes were up, he spurred the horse away from the direction Pat had taken, circled the house and moved in an arc and would gradually meet the flight path of Pat who was headed towards a particularly crumpled stretch of grass, bush, thicket and trees which he recalled so well and the main features of which were obvious in the crepuscular gloom. So began the most bizarre hunt that this well-hunted stretch of Irish countryside had ever witnessed.

"Pat was confident to start with. He knew the ground well and he could move very quietly for such a big man. True to his word, he kept the sash on and sought dense foliage and sheltering dips and hollows which would hide it from view. At the start, he had conditioned himself to avoid danger which was approaching from behind. Soon, though, he heard Lucifer moving along ahead and to one side of him. Damn! He'd made the mistake of assuming that James would rely on his initial movements to plot his pursuit. He crashed through a stretch of bushes which he knew opened up onto an open grassy stretch. As he came out onto the grass, a small herd of fallow deer erupted in alarm and set off at a high-speed gallop towards the small wood on the far side of the plain. Pat joined them and reached the wood almost at the same time. There, he fell to the ground and rolled into a ball in the tall grass.

"For a moment, he thought his ruse had succeeded. Lucifer, caught up in the excitement of a chase, followed the deer at a fast gallop, but James reined him in and, standing up in his stirrups, scanned the grassy plain. From his high vantage point, he soon spotted Pat and turned the stallion in his direction. Pat stood up and ran as fast as he had ever done towards a sunken path he knew lay ahead, hearing the thudding hooves of Lucifer gaining on him. On the path, he ran until he came across a fallen oak, the splayed branches of which blocked the entire path, from steep bank to steep bank. For a moment, he thought of scrambling through the branches, where the horse could never have followed, but something, perhaps pride, stopped him. He turned and faced his pursuers.

"James reined in the horse for a moment and then drove his spurs into the heaving sides and lashed the sweating flanks with his whip. Lucifer lunged forward, foam dripping from his mouth and splashing James. Pat stood straight up and, facing the huge stallion and its demented rider, held out his arms as if to welcome the collision. With James screaming in his ear and the spurs and whip goading him onwards, Lucifer, at the last possible moment, recognised the one man who had treated him with kindness and tried to leap over him. He succeeded in clearing Pat, except for his right rear hoof which connected with Pat's brain pan and shattered it like an eggshell. The momentum carried the stallion in amongst the oak branches, one of which broke his neck, killing him instantly, and James's death was a split second behind his; his torso was lanced right through by a splintered branch which tore his heart and one lung from his chest as his body tumbled on and spread its gore on the twisted branches of the oak."

***

There was a long silence as Curly absorbed the grim tale and James took a long, slow drink of brandy.

"My mother didn't live long after that. She had heard the full tale from the butler, whom she sacked because she couldn't bear to have him in the house after the slaughter. On her death bed about six months later, she more or less admitted that she had loved both men totally and she wasn't really sure which of them had been my father."

He drained the glass, stood up and stirred the fire. Then he looked into the embers before turning to Curly.

"So, Collins. You are looking at a walking encapsulation of Ireland's history, and there are thousands such as I who are products of a tortured land. Enjoy your travels and don't get involved in the history. Goodnight. You'll be called in the morning for breakfast."

Curly nodded and left the last of the Rathbones staring into a dying fire.

5

The town

He meandered vaguely westward and southward, not really caring about the journey, or, to be honest, the destination. He slowed as he came to a small signpost snuggled comfortably in among the brambles and stopped to read the two signs. *Beal na Bla* was five miles ahead, and a town called Ballymalloy was eight.

At the town of *Beal na Bla* itself, he stopped to fill up the Buick and took the admiration of the pump operator as his due.

"That's an amazing bloody car, that."

"Yes. It is."

"I'm not sure I have enough petrol to fill it," said the operator. "Have you it switched off? I think it's gaining on me."

"I'll tell you when to stop."

In fact, he had to watch his spending since his funds were getting low. The operator stopped pumping and extracted the hose. A small drop of petrol landed on the car and he hurriedly whipped out a rag and wiped it off.

"Sorry. I won't charge you for that."

Curly pulled a note out of his slim billfold.

"There. Keep the change."

"Thanks, ould son. That should get you to the next corner." He nodded at the spectacular grill. "Ye'd need a toothbrush for that thing."

"Yes. They supplied one but I lost it."

The operator looked at him blankly.

"I thought I'd stay a while in Ballymalloy. Is there any work there?"

The operator seemed stunned that an American with such a huge car would want work, so he took some time to answer.

"Well, there's a factory there. They might be wanting someone."

"Okay. Thanks."

"You're welcome."

He slammed the hose back into the bowser and Curly slipped into the Buick and drove away slowly. The operator looked after the car. "Quare folk, the Yanks. Amazing bloody car, though."

***

Curly didn't spend much time at the Michael Collins memorial. There wasn't much to see there and only one small plaque, badly weather stained, showing a map of the ambush and a few words on the event. He perused it and the massive Celtic cross with Collins' name in Gaelic and stood a while on the brick plinth. Once more, he was impressed at the quietness of the Irish country roads and the bright greenness of the landscapes they meandered through. He would stay a while in Ballymalloy and then head homewards, although he wasn't quite sure where the 'home' would be. His uncle had been the last of his relatives that he knew of, and he was sure he wasn't going to seek out any more in Ireland. What would he do if he found them? Impose on them? Intrude into their lives? No. He'd go wherever his road led him. But looking at this winding road, with its ubiquitous hedgerows, he realised that he would have forgotten which way he had been travelling if it weren't for the Buick parked at the roadside. Maybe he should use the car as his lodestar and drive it wherever it was pointing until it stopped running. Where *was* he headed?

Ballymalloy. Maybe his destiny lay in a town that was important enough to have an official signpost pointing at it. He went heavily down the steps and walked to the car.

It didn't take long to reach the sign that marked the entrance to Ballymalloy, and he drove slowly along the main street, not knowing that his passing had caused ripples among the denizens. One such was Mary MacBride, whose head emerged through the neck of a dress she was trying on in the town's only dressmaker's shop as the Buick was passing. Minnie, the dressmaker, mouth full of pins, joined her at the window and shared a sigh as they watched the car pass by. Further along, Artie Bell was carrying a sheet of metal across the yard of the factory as the car passed. He stopped, hawked, spat and glared at the car with wishful envy. At the church that faced out onto the main street, Father O'Grady paused as he crossed himself with holy water from the font at the door. He looked after the car as it passed, was distracted and walked into a pillar. A keen observer with lip reading abilities would have identified the short word he uttered as one not befitting a man in holy orders. In a tiny grave-yard next to the church, Joy de Burg, an old woman in wheelchair, was tossing flowers on a well-tended grave when the car passed. She waved at the car and Curly waved back. She smiled as if remembering something pleasant. As the Buick drew level with the only hotel in Ballymalloy an elderly couple, Mr and Mrs Smith, was crossing the road way ahead of him. Mrs. Smith grabbed her partner's arm and scurried across to the hotel as if her life was in mortal danger. Curly soon reached another Ballymalloy sign, facing the other way. Small as it was, he felt that this was a place he could lose himself in. He passed the sign, did a six-point turn and started to drive slowly back along the what must be the main street, looking at the various buildings, none of which had any aesthetic merit but collectively that were the quintessence of a typical Irish town and dispensed a sense of rightness for the uneventful time and the unremarkable place.

One man in Ballymalloy watched the car pass with a great intensity and wonderment as he leaned on a massive delivery bike. He was twisted and bent but strangely agile for all that. They called him Smack in the town because of a nervous mannerism he had if anybody spoke sharply to him or if he felt threatened by a sudden, angry gesture. He would duck his head and raise his shoulders and mutter, "Don't smack. Don't smack." He talked to himself all the time, in a low mutter which was audible only if one stood close to him and concentrated. Unfortunately, very few people did concentrate on anything Smack muttered, so he muttered away in a strange stream-of-consciousness way which was, actually, worthy of being listened to.

"Big. So big. A chariot. Must be the biggest car in the world. Bet it could do hundreds of miles an hour. The man who drives it? Must be a magician. Bet it can go faster than my bike, even going downhill to Lennon's farm on the Mallow Road. First farm. White gates. Big dogs that bark. Bark! Don't smack. Man in the car smiled at me! Nice man. I'll show him the way. Catch him. There. Pass him. Wave him on. This way! This way!"

Waving and wobbling, he escorted the Buick along the street until he came to the factory. Here, he swerved in through the gate, ringing his bell frantically. To his delight, the Buick replied with a melodious honk on the horn.

The Ballymalloy Hotel was like every small main road hotel in every small Irish town. The façade was strangely, perhaps even deliberately, nondescript. Flat and self-deprecating, it lurked at the top of a few steps which led to a raised pavement barely wide enough for a person to walk along. The building crouched above this pavement and barely qualified as a two-story edifice. The ground floor windows were strangely truncated as if they feared intruding into the upper floor space. The sharply angled roof was tiled in dull, non-coloured slate, that muted to invisibility any hint of blue which made the effort to appear in the Ballymalloy skies. The entrance at the top of the steps, but not really in line with them, was low and boasted double doors, neither of which, because they were crammed into a constricted width, were adequate enough to admit any normal sized person carrying a single suitcase and, since only one of these doors was ever left open, every guest had to sidle through the gap and stumble down a little step into the reception area which boasted a reception desk obviously built for much larger premises. Consequently, each guest had a skewed and disorienting introduction to the welcoming charms of Ballymalloy's premier hospitality locus. None of this dampened the appetites of Mr and Mrs Smith as they made their way to their usual window table in the dining room for their invariable afternoon tea. Freddie Flannigan, the well-built owner of the hotel, hastened to manoeuvre the chair for Mrs Smith and slid it in as she took her seat. He moved the tea things on the table into alignment and braced himself.

"Where's the flowers, Freddie?" she said, glad to have found some fault. "When your mother was alive, God rest her soul, there were always flowers on this table."

"There were flowers on your table yesterday," said Freddie weakly.

"There used to be flowers every day."

"Mary's bringing the flowers, Mrs Smith."

Mrs Smith was examining her cutlery and, with a sharp intake of breath, started to vigorously polish the knife.

"This used to be the best hotel in Ballymalloy," she told her reflection in the EPNS.

"It's the only hotel in Ballymalloy..." said Mr Smith, "...dear."

"It could be the last hotel too," said Freddie, fending off Mrs Smith's indignation at her spouse's interjection. Mr Smith gave him a sympathetic smile.

"That's the problem. No competition," said Mrs Smith. "Smith likes flowers."

"Aah. Oh." said Mr Smith. "I suppose I do."

"But they make me sneeze," said Mrs Smith, now that the cutlery was fit to be used. Mr Smith leaned towards Freddie.

"Saw you at the bank yesterday. Being difficult, are they?"

"Very!' said Freddie as he caught sight of the Buick. "Will you look at that car! I hope it's a tourist."

"Tourists, how are you!" grumbled Mrs Smith. "Have they no homes to go to? That's the car that nearly killed us. Didn't it, Smith?"

"Aah. Oh. Did it?"

"Smith nearly had a heart attack. It's no fun walking around Ballymalloy anymore. Smith?"

"No! It's not!" said her uxorious one with an unexpected vigour that elicited a surprised look from Mrs Smith.

Aah. Oh. I mean... not with cars and... everything."

Freddie thought it was time to bring in the tea, so he made his escape to the kitchen at the back of the spacious dining room. By taking that route, he missed the first contact between Curly Collins and Mary MacBride, which was to have serious and interesting consequences for them both. Having parked the Buick outside the entrance to the hotel, Curly took a suitcase and the box of records from the car and ascended the outside steps to the front door. He staggered, for the first of many times, as he stepped down into the reception area. In doing so, he collided with Mary, who was hurrying towards the dining room carrying a small vase of flowers which flew from her hands and shattered on the wooden floor. Mary's peal of laughter assuaged his guilt somewhat.

"What'll you think of us all?" she asked as she bent down to retrieve the flowers. "Knocking our guests about – and it's not even hunting season."

Curly set the suitcase on the floor and bent down to help her, with the box still under his arm.

"Season or not, If I am to be knocked about, it couldn't be done in a nicer way."

Mary noticed that he was trying to peer down the front of her dress, so she pulled her shoulders back and gathered up the flowers while allowing Curly to collect the bits of the vase and one of the flowers which had fallen from the bunch. She was suddenly all business.

"You'll be wanting a room. Do you mind signing in?"

She took the bits of glass from him and moved behind the desk. Turning the register towards him, she threw the vase pieces in a bin and watched as he placed the box on the desk and signed the register. Holding the flowers, she craned to see what he was writing.

"Will you be staying long, Mr... Collins?"

"Call me Curly. That depends on the action."

"Oh, we have sodality every Wednesday evening, Mr Collins." She caught his puzzlement. "It's devotional."

"I was thinking of something—"

"I'll reserve a seat for you if you like."

"More exciting."

"Near the pulpit."

"Something with—"

"Father O'Grady is great value. What sort of room are you wanting?"

Outmanoeuvred, Curly sighed. "The cheapest you've got."

She selected a key and handed it to him. "There you are, Mr Collins. No. 12. It's small but comfortable."

Freddie came through the reception, carrying a keg of beer with ease. He caught the dynamic and wasn't pleased, so he slowed down as he passed. Curly tried again.

"A man could get lost in Ballymalloy. I need somebody to show me around."

"Oh, we don't do tours. Only dinner, bed and breakfast. No. 12. Turn right at the top of the stairs."

"Everything all right, Mary?"

"Game-ball, Mr Flannigan. Mr Collins is just going to his room."

In the resultant stand-off, Curly shrugged and laid the single flower on the desk directly in front of Mary. He picked up the box, collected his suitcase and moved to the stairs. Mary and Freddie looked at the flower for a moment before Mary picked it up and added it to the other flowers. Curly stopped and turned back. Freddie stepped in front of him.

"Welcome, Mr Collins. I'm Freddy Flannigan, the owner. I'm sure you'll find all is satisfactory."

"Any work around here?" Curly asked.

"Your best bet is the factory, just down the road. Mostly unskilled jobs."

"Thanks." As he climbed the stairs, he overheard the subdued conversation at the desk.

"How's it at the bank, Mr Flannigan?" Mary asked.

"Not good. They're calling in the loan."

"They can't!"

They've given me two months. That's it."

"AHEM!" This came from the dining room.

"Mrs Smith!" exclaimed Mary as she rushed off to find another vase. "She be spitting fishhooks."

Curly went to No. 12 and entered. It was a small room with a single bed, a chair, a precarious wardrobe, a marble-topped chest of drawers with a floral jug in a floral washbasin and a neat row of thick drinking glasses on it. The window looked out onto the street. He threw the suitcase on the bed, which sagged alarmingly, and placed the box on top of the wardrobe. Taking a hip flask from his pocket and a glass from the washstand, he tipped a generous tot into it and walked to the window. Looking out over Ballymalloy, he sipped his drink and thought about how far away he was from Broadway.

There *was* work at the factory. An unexpected and urgent order had come in for the drilling and spray painting of a large quantity of mild steel panels, so, when Curly appeared next morning, the manager hired him on the spot under the watchful eye of Artie, who considered himself the foreman of the factory, although he was merely the longest-serving employee there. The entire workforce consisted of the manager – a nephew of the ever-absent owner, Artie; and Smack with the enormous bike which he could ride fast, unless the package or fabrication in the voluminous basket at the front was particularly heavy or unwieldly. Like thousands of delivery 'boys' before or since, this man was totally unaware of the initial impact the bike had on the world of commerce, especially in outlying areas and suburbs. Supplanting the horse-drawn delivery waggons of the preceding decades, the modest vehicle on which the passenger was the power source brought a welcome degree of convenience to purveyors and customers alike. Smack and his bike went boldly where no motorised vehicle dared or cared to go. Smack and his bike were welcome in the houses, cottages and main street businesses and relied upon in all weathers, and it was a rare day when he didn't receive some food or a glass of rich milk for his trouble.

This miniscule staff had not prevented the manager from buying a time clock which he mounted on the wall just inside the factory's main shed and in direct line of sight from his office. Since Artie invariably ate his lunch sandwiches on the bench under the time clock, sharing the crusts with Smack, all three could see each other at almost any time of the day. This rendered the practical value of the clock of singular insignificance, but it gave the manager a sense of being in control, and if either of his employees failed to clock in immediately upon entering the yard, he would rap on the window and gesticulate wildly.

Sometime, indeed, when there was little or no work to do, Artie would cycle into the yard in the morning at his usual time and deliberately not clock in but would saunter in and out of the shed on make-believe business, pointedly keeping his eyes off the manager's window until he could sense that the manager was leaving his office to come and berate him, whereupon he would extract his card and clock in with a flourish. The manager would return to his office frustrated, and Artie would be in a good humour for most of the morning. Such were the daily goings-on at the only factory in Ballymalloy, but the unexpected new business and Curly's employment brought some changes to the establishment.

"This is mild steel," said Artie, as he waved a sheet of the material and a stiff paper template at Curly. "It is exactly one sixteenth of an inch thick. I use this template to mark the exact position of the holes that you are going to drill with that drill over there. Now that drill has a bit that's exactly three eights of an inch. Have you got that?"

"It'd be hard not to get it."

"What?"

"It's hard, but I get it."

"This is where this template comes in. The holes have to be exactly in the right place. Otherwise—"

"They won't line up with the holes in the other bits of mild steel they're to be joined to."

Artie was a bit put out by the fact that Curly should know this esoteric fact, so he had to assert his authority.

"I've been doing this job for over ten years."

"Is that all?"

"What do you mean?"

"You seem to know so much about it."

Artie swelled a little.

"I do. Believe me, I do."

Later that evening, Mary and Minnie were walking towards the hotel when a garish notice in the front window caught Minnie's eye.

"Will you look at that," she said.

"I put it up there myself this morning. They're putting them up all around West Cork. In every town."

The poster screamed in primary colours:

GREAT NATIONAL **JAZZ** DANCE COMPETITION

*We're looking for the best jazz dancers in Ireland. Winners of local heats will travel to Dublin for the finals AND MAY STAR IN THE WORLD-FAMOUS SHOW, **JAZZ**, FRESH FROM ITS BROADWAY SUCCESS.*

Auditions at the Ballymalloy Hotel, Friday 14th Register now!!!!!

"It's a pity it's not jigs and reels," said Mary. "I'd stand a chance there, seeing I was the *rince* queen of Killorglin?"

"*Rince* indeed! With your arms and back straight and the teacher telling you not to kick so high you'll show your knickers. Jay! Give us a few steps."

Mary obliged with a few very deft steps of a reel and bowed as Minnie clapped lavishly. They were about to enter the hotel when the Buick pulled up beside them and Curly blew the hooter. The girls turned to face him.

"Hi, girls. Can I give you a lift somewhere?" Curly asked.

Minnie was about to say yes when Mary spoke.

"Sure, I'd get a nosebleed if I climbed up into that yolk. Thanks anyway, Mr Collins."

They both turned and entered the hotel. Curly stroked the upholstery.

"Yolk! I'll get her onto your back seat yet, old buddy."

He drove the Buick down the street without any idea of where he was going. As he passed the graveyard, he thought of his uncle and decided he would walk around the graves in some sort of unfocussed tribute to him and his General Motors bequest, so he pulled up outside the gates and got out of the car.

Inside the graveyard, Joy de Burg in her wheelchair had stopped next to a gravestone inscribed with the name 'Joseph M. Murphy'. She was tossing some flowers one by one onto the grave but turned around towards the street as she heard the Buick stop. She saw Curly get out of the car and walk slowly among the gravestones, inspecting them with a distracted air. She sat so still that Curly saw her only at the last minute.

"That's the car that has the whole of Ballymalloy going ga-ga. I'm Joy de Burg."

She held her hand out and Curly stopped and took it gently in his.

"Curly Collins," he said as he released it.

"Do you have somebody buried here? Lots of Americans think – hope – they have."

"Cemetery tourists?"

"Something like that. It's funny how the New World looks for its roots in the Old World."

"Not surprising, since we all came from here."

"You've got one of your ancestors commemorated near here."

"I have, yes."

"And did you pay your respects at *Beal na Bla*"

"I did."

"Why?"

"Because my uncle thought fit to leave Ireland after the assassination."

"Good. Who was your uncle?"

"Nobody of any consequence. He just felt that the Ireland that was emerging wasn't the place he wanted to live in."

"And he was right. Thank you."

This was in response to Curly's move to assist her in getting her wheelchair of the grass and onto the gravel path. "Every woman in Ireland was in love with Collins, the Big Fella."

"Were you?"

"Of course. It was the flatness of the landscape. Who was left but the Ould Hoor, de Valera? So you've nobody here?"

He was thinking how certain attributes and nicknames had become part of the lexicon attached to heroes in all countries, such as George Washington's indomitable honesty, and had to be referred to when talking about them.

"No. I just like graveyards. They're so... peaceful," he finally said.

"And sad. There's a lot of dreams buried here among the bones," said Joy as Curly pushed her chair up onto the cement pavement that led to the gate. She stopped as the car came into full view. "I'm thinking that'd be a grand, comfortable vehicle to drive around in. Especially on a soft day like this." She looked up at him expectantly.

Curly knew how outmanoeuvred he was.

"Would you like a drive?"

"How very unexpected of you. I haven't seen the Gap of Dunloe in ages."

He helped her into the car firmly and decorously and installed her on the front seat. He then stowed the wheelchair in the trunk. As he got back into the driving seat, Joy was running her fingers over the faux wood panel of the dashboard.

"A lovely bit of venereal, that. You must feel very important driving a car like this."

"Well, it's the best car America ever made."

"And you're used to the best?"

"I was once." He started the car. "Which way?"

"Drive slowly along the main street, so they can all see me and then just follow your nose."

As the car pulled away, Joy kept up a running commentary.

"There's Father O'Grady, a saint of a man if a little lenient in his penances. There's the Smiths in the hotel as usual at this time of day. I don't suppose she ever cooks at home. Poor Smith, he

47

doesn't know whether he's on foot or on horseback. Repenting at leisure, he is – for nearly fifty years. I see Minnie's making a smashing new dress for Mary. There's the factory, the industrial hub of Ballymalloy. How's the work there?"

"It's hardly science."

"Of course it's not! Science stops in Dublin. West Cork is still in the pre-industrial age. Watch out!"

Smack on his delivery bike swerved in front of the Buick as he made a skidded turn into the factory, and Curly had to brake sharply to avoid hitting him.

"Poor fellow. Nobody knows where he came from, but he acts as if he owns the streets. And the whole town loves him and looks after him. He does some bits of work for me. We get along well, so we do. Now straight on until I tell you."

Joy sat back and luxuriated in the ride. In the soft light of early evening, the Buick drove north and west into a purple and pink sky. The narrow gravel road wound its way, in the absent-minded manner that all Irish country roads have. Through pristine grasslands and low craggy outcrops of mottled rocks it meandered as if this was the only, the preordained, the historically inevitable way to one of the glories of South-West Ireland. Slowly, with a smug sense of geological drama, the greenish-bronze loom of the sandstone Purple Mountain and, a little beyond, the MacGillycuddy Reeks mountain range beckoned, and the road plunged through a chiaroscuro of mosses, ferns, low shrubs and wildflowers, all of which were iridescent in the rays of the low sun. There were bogs here and clumps of the sacred yew that had sheltered and sanctified ancient practices. But when the road soared, topped a rise and approached the first of the five lakes that pearled their way through the Gap, the effect was physical, and Curly stopped the Buick and tried to absorb it all. The beauty was gemlike, but scale was the first thing that impressed him. In his journeys through America, he had driven through some spectacular scenery, but here it all seemed so… people-sized. At the far end of the first lake was a small bridge with a single arch in the middle of its reach.

"Stop at the Wishing Bridge, please, Curly."

Across from the bridge he eased the Buick onto a patch of gravel and sand and stopped where Joy could look at the bridge and pellucid water as the light slowly departed the valley. He saw that she was deeply moved and that tears gathered in the corners of her eyes, so he stopped the car and got out, leaving her with her memories. A small pony and trap passed him slowly. The driver touched the brim of his hat with a horny hand and tickled the rump of the pony with a long whip. The pony carried on at an even pace, ignoring the affectionate whip contact. Curly touched his forehead and nodded as the man whispered "Soft day" and passed, looking at the Buick with idle interest. Curly watched as Joy's mind came back into focus. She sat up a little straighter, sighed deeply and looked around for him. He approached.

"I've needed that for many a long year," Joy said as he got back into the driving seat. "Will you be able to turn here or must you go as far as the town?"

"Should be able to make it if we both inhale deeply."

And make it he did, with a ten-point turn. She smiled at him as he straightened the car on the road, facing the way they had come.

"Good exercise, driving this car."

"Yes. Even with power steering. It wasn't designed for these roads."

She reached across and laid a hand lightly on his sleeve.

"Thank you, Curly. That was an important visit."

He nodded and drove on.

***

49

It was night before they got back to Ballymalloy, and Curly parked the Buick as close to Joy's cottage as he could. Getting her out of the car and into her wheelchair was the work of a moment, as was wheeling her up and through the front door. As they approached the front door, Smack slipped out and disappeared into the night.

"Goodnight, Smack. Thanks," Joy called out into the darkness. "He's just dropped off some supplies I ordered. He's a grand man."

Going into her small lounge was a trip back fifty years. The décor, the furniture and the knick-knacks were high Victorian, and every surface – and there were many – was laden with photographs in gilt, silver, ornamental wood, engraved glass and enamel frames, as if each image was precious and deserving of the best of display. As indeed they were. All the important events and times in Joy's long life were there. Joy wheeled herself over to a highly ornate cabinet and dropped down the front. A neat array of bottles was displayed.

"That's flushed out the old brain cells. Sherry?"

"Thank you, yes," said Curly as he picked up a prominently displayed photograph of a woman in a wide-skirted dance gown. It was a younger Joy. "This is you!"

"In my dancing days. Yes. We had dancing every weekend, all over the county. Travel miles, we would. The men so smart. The women so lovely. Everyone graceful."

He picked up another photograph of Joy with a tall and handsome man in full white tie and tails. Joy wheeled herself over to him with a slim crystal glass in her hand.

"The last of the Amontillado, I'm sorry to say." She looked at the photograph. "Joe Murphy. My best partner."

She wheeled herself back to the cabinet and picked up another glass. "I'll tell you about him sometime. When I'm not so tired. *Slainte.*"

"*Slainte,*" he said and they drank appreciatively. As they were savouring the rich flavour, the front door rattled and Mary burst through the hall and into the lounge. She carried some paper bags and was clearly annoyed to see Curly.

"Hello, dear. We've just been for a lovely drive," said Joy.

"I'm sure. I'll just put these in the kitchen." She stormed out and Curly finished his drink.

"Thank you, Joy," he said loudly. "You're the first person to make me feel welcome in Ballymalloy."

A slamming cupboard door in the kitchen indicated that the intended recipient had heard him. He kissed the hand that Joy held out to him and took gentle leave of her. Out in the Buick, as he started the engine, he glanced back at the cottage in time to see the curtain behind the door window twitch open and Mary's face appeared briefly. He smiled and drove away. After parking the Buick in the yard at the rear of the hotel, he walked to the front door, to which he had the key. The notice for the *Jazz* auditions caught his eye and he stopped in shock. Jesus! Was there no respite from the show? Not even in this excuse for a town? In his mind's eye, he could still clearly see the stony faces of the two producers as they sent his pride and career into freefall. He would be well out of this town before the auditions. He couldn't bear to think about even being in the same vicinity as them. It would be too painful and damaging to his ego.

**

Ballymalloy slept under a cloud-straggled moon. The west wind, with the scent of the ocean in its gusts, stirred the waiting trees and sent the weaker leaves tumbling onto the uneven paths and the tarmacked road. It sought out the badly nailed tiles on the houses in the main street and rattled them disapprovingly. It slammed the windows left carelessly open and whistled in through the ill-fitting doors like a lonesome spirit. It made the blue lamp in front of the church altar flicker and blew out the stubs of the candles lit by hopeful or rememberful parishioners who had dropped in to seek a little solace in the dim, echoing shadows, the smell of incense and warm candlewax. And the people of Ballymalloy slept the sleep of the under-stimulated in the nondescript town just akimbo of one of the world-famous tourist routes to the natural wonders of South-West Ireland.

In the yard of the hotel, the Buick clicked softly as it cooled from the night ride and, on his bed, Curly clicked his teeth against the glass of whisky that he was sipping as he thought of Mary and the fact that he hadn't had a woman for several long months and wondered what it would be like to deflower her because she *would* be a virgin. There was no other option in this priest-ridden place. One benign priest in a place halfway between a village and a town hardly made it priest-ridden, but he had heard tales of the ubiquity of the sanctimonious throughout Ireland. Then, in spite of himself, the *Jazz* show intruded and his mild tumescence disappeared as he grappled with the lost opportunity.

Meanwhile, Mary tossed and turned in her virginal bed and wondered what it would be like to whirl through the countryside in the Buick with all the windows down, even if it *was* Curly driving. The cheek of him! Making a pass at her. Was it a pass, though? Trying to see down her dress was hardly a pass, but offering her a ride in his car definitely qualified. She had turned him down. Maybe she had been too hasty. Would he ask her again? Probably. He was full of himself, so he was! Good-looking too. Ah well. No use in being sorry. She drifted off into a discontented and fitful sleep.

Minnie had no such reservations. She'd be into that car like a rat up a drain. Didn't matter if he turned out to be all hands. She could handle that sort of behaviour, especially in such a car. Her sleep turned out to be discontented too but for different reasons.

Freddie tossed and turned and cursed the bank.

Joy was dancing in her dreams, looking and feeling young and basking in the firm, confident arms of a good dancing partner.

6

The outing

The morning came, as mornings are wont to do, and Ballymalloy shrugged off its small-hours' fears, phobias and apprehensions and faced a new day which, like all new days, was redolent of brighter thoughts and better things to come. The dining room at the hotel was bustling with its few passing commercial travellers, its long-term patrons and its regular local trade, comprising those townsfolk who couldn't be bothered messing up their own kitchens with the usual copious antemeridian indulgence – THE FRY. Greasy, glutinous and traditionally sacrosanct, the Irish breakfast, like all peasant dishes, was a serious meal; fried eggs that were firm and more than ready to void their golden contents at the prod of a fork; bacon that was well cured, curly and crisp; sausages (pork of course) that were preferably bursting at either end; fried potato slices that were crisp around the edge and creamily soft in the centre; a slice or two of tomato greased all the way through, and the glory of the Irish table – fried bread, in thick, lard-laden, irregular slices that would act either as a subsidiary plate for the eggs or a sop for the greasy and flavoursome residue. All washed down with very dark, almost coagulant tea, brewed to hell and gone, strong enough to free the rusted wheels on a railway bogie and rendered even more costive by unpasteurised milk and heaped spoonfuls of sugar. The radio was playing, but nobody was listening to the cultivated tones of the announcer's Received Pronunciation:

"And bringing this programme of American Jazz on the BBC's Light Programme to a close is *I Can't Get Started* by Bunny Berrigan. Recorded in 1937."

Curly was sipping tea and watching Mary dispensing meals on the tables as the liquid trumpet notes cascaded over the diners' heads. Mary started to move with the music at the dispensing table next to the kitchen and he watched with interest. She moved well but he could see that she was not *with* the music in a meaningful way. He was thinking that a bit of coaching would not go amiss when she gathered an armful of plates, descended on his table and placed a laden plate in front of him.

"Eggs over easy?" he asked.

"Over and easy as you'll get them this side of the Atlantic."

She moved on to the Smiths' table and deposited a plate in front of Mrs Smith.

"There you are, Mrs Smith. Bacon crispy, sausages soft, eggs hard. Just the way you like them."

Mrs Smith grunted and pointed at the sugar bowl.

"What's them blocks?" she asked.

Mary put a plate in front of Mr Smith.

"The potatoes are just the way you like them, Mr Smith."

"Thank you, Mary. Lumps, my dear."

"What?"

"They're sugar lumps, my dear. It's the way now."

"Has all the goodness squeezed out too, I dare say. I'll have my sugar in the usual way, thank you very much. Lumps!"

Mary scooped up the sugar bowl and moved away, stopping a moment at another table.

"Porridge all right, sir?"

"Perfect, thanks," said the man addressed.

"No lumps?"

"Nary a one."

"Lumps!" said Mrs Smith again.

As the music picked up pace, she started to move with it, serving food, scooping up plates, opening drawers in the central server and closing them with her hips. *That's much better*, thought Curly as she moved instinctively and well.

"Mary," shouted Mrs Smith, "I don't know why we have to listen to that noise. It's giving Smith a headache."

Mr Smith, who was nodding in time with the music, suddenly looked up and changed his expression to disapproving. Mary approached Curly, rolling her eyes, and filled his cup from the copious teapot.

"There. That'll put hairs on your chest."

"Busy, hey?"

"This is nothing. Wait 'til the drovers come next week. They'll all be bellowing and bucking, just like their cattle."

Freddie came bustling in and beckoned her over to the side.

"The bookings are pouring in for the dance auditions. We'll fill the house next door too. It needs a good cleaning there. Maybe a lick of paint too."

"Don't worry. We'll handle that."

"I'll see the bank again today."

"That's good."

"Freddie!" It was Mrs Smith again. "Smith wants you to turn that music off."

"Right away, Mrs Smith," said Freddie as he hurried into reception. The music stopped and an Irish voice came in its place.

"… frontal system crossing the country from east to west. Now here is the shipping forecast for the coast from Erris Head to Carnsore Point… "

After breakfast, Curly made his reluctant way through the rain to the factory. He held in his hand a newspaper-wrapped package which was fast turning to pulp. As he turned in through the gate, Smack appeared out of the gloom of the shed.

"Hi, Smack. Some fried bread for you."

Smack grabbed the package and disappeared into the darkness muttering,

"Fried bread. Lard. From pigs it's made. A bit cold now. Sticks to your teeth and the top of your mouth. Good, though. Hold it there until it warms a bit then it slides down, greasy all the way. Eat the middle first. Then the crusts. Got them at the convent – Don't smack – but dry there. Not like this. Bump. In the belly. Feels good."

Curly was half listening, trying to decipher the muttering, when Artie loomed into view, carrying a steel sheet.

"The last few, before we start spray painting them."

Curly grabbed the sheet and winced as it snagged his fingers. He placed it on the small pile next to his bench and examined his hands. He had always taken care of them and his nails, but this drilling had messed them up badly, not only because of the jagged edges but also because the drill bit produced thin, sharp curls of steel that burrowed into his flesh, no matter how careful he was.

"Why are the edges so fucking rough?" he asked.

"Probably because they will be fitted into some frame that will cover the edges. It's better than galvanised tin. That really cuts you to shreds."

"And the spray painting?"

"A shitty green, they want. Oh, you'll love that."

But Curly knew that he wouldn't and he was right. For two full days, he hung four sheets on a long, spiked beam that traversed a badly ventilated annex at the back of the shed and, face mask in place, walked along them, spraying one side of each with a hand-pumped spray gun which was fed through a long hose from a drum of the paint to one side of the spraying area. He soon got the hang of it, moving the nozzle from side to side with an even motion, ensuring that each spray overlapped the one above evenly, so that there was no discernible difference in the thickness of the paint. His first few efforts were not very successful, but Artie was forgiving, saying that nobody would notice. Artie used two clumsily contrived lifting devices with spikes protruding from the centres to transfer each sprayed sheet to another spiked beam to dry. So, they went on until all the sheets were sprayed and dry. Then Artie led him to a primitive press at another corner of this capacious shed. On it, he placed one of the sprayed sheets.

"See them score marks?" he said, indicating two small scratches on each side of the steel sheet. "I'll do the marking. You line up the marks with the edge of the press and you bend it at right angles with this lever. It's easy."

"Why don't you bend the sheets before spraying them?" Curly asked.

"Why should we do that? I'd be more work for us."

"The bending will probably crack the paint. It will certainly weaken it and probably rust will form along the line."

"That's not our problem. Our problem is to get all the sheets finished before the end of the week. Now get bending."

Pondering the latent faults that were built into this form of fabrication, Curly got bending and could see again and again how damaged the fresh paint became along the inflicted fault line. He got through quite a few sheets before Artie decided that the factory had stopped for lunch, and the three employees clocked out and sat down on various benches to eat the lunches that Curly and Artie had brought with them. Smack had brewed up a tin can of very strong tea and served it in tin cups to the others. He sat on a separate bench and waited for scraps from the two men. Nor was he disappointed. Artie passed over one of his three rough-hewn sandwiches which Smack demolished in four gigantic bites and dispatched down his gullet with a speed that threatened to tear his scrawny upper thorax apart. They were washed down by enormous gulps of tea which sent his Adam's apple bounding up and down like a bony yo-yo. Then he belched dramatically and looked at Curly, who passed over one of his more delicate sandwiches, prepared in the hotel's kitchen. It too disappeared with commendable dispatch, and having sent it on its way, via a veritable Niagara of tea, through his alimentary canal, Smack belched again, nodded his thanks and disappeared in the darker regions of the shed to snooze away the rest of his lunch break. Curly waited until the food was gone, the wrappings tossed into a waste bin next to the door and Artie's pipe ignited before he spoke.

"I've been thinking," he said, and Artie turned to face him, "about the making of things. Take the Buick, for instance."

"A remarkable car, that."

"It is. They've been making to for over ten years now. It has Christ knows how many moving parts."

"It's a marvel. Got to hand it to the Yanks. The know how to make things."

"The thing is, it's well engineered."

"True."

"I've been watching you, Artie. It seems you can make anything."

Artie looked sideways at him in a suspicious manner.

"Yeah," he said at last. "I suppose I can."

"Where did you learn it all?"

"I dunno. I suppose I just picked it up as I went along."

"Come on. You must have studied somewhere?"

"Never. My old man was good with things. I used to watch him and he'd let me do things when I was in the mood."

"And when you started to earn a living?"

"I used to go to the various workshops and factories around the towns and just ask for a job. If I could prove I could use the various tools and machines they had, I got a job."

"And if you couldn't?"

"I never came across a bit of machinery in places like this...

" he looked around and paused, "… that I couldn't get the hang of in minutes. I'd look at it for a while and work out what it was supposed to do and then I could do it. Every time."

"On another level, the Buick—"

"Ah, that's another matter now. Entirely."

"It is but I reckon that if you saw the assembly line in a Buick factory, you'd know exactly what was going on and could work at any part of that assembly line after looking at it for a minute or two."

"Ah. Go on!"

"I'm serious. Ford was the first to break the making of a motor car into simple steps that any man could do."

In spite of himself, Artie was intrigued and drawn deeply into the conversation.

"Each step is carried out at a different part of the line as the thing that's being made moves along. Take those fucking sheets, for instance. Somebody flattened the mild steel into huge sheets one sixteenth of an inch thick, and then the next man cut them into sheets of the right size. Then they were sent on to have those fucking holes drilled in them and the next man bent them and the next sprayed them. Then the next—"

"Hold on now. They were sprayed before they were bent."

"In a proper manufacturing process, they wouldn't be. They would be bent first."

"But the whole… assembly… thing would have to stop while they dried. What would happen then?'

"Good thinking Artie. In a proper assembly line, the sprayed sheets would be given time to dry and then fed back into, maybe, another assembly line while the frames were brought in and cut and drilled and made ready for the sheets to be bolted in. The thing is, the proper sequence was worked out beforehand for every single part so that nothing would hold up the assembly of the final product."

Artie was silent, absorbing all this, and Curly could see he was working it out properly in his head. He sipped his tea and waited silently. Finally, Artie spoke.

"I see what you mean. It would all go much quicker."

"And cheaper. It's called mass production, and Henry Ford was the first to get it right. He had watched the mass production of beef in the Chicago stockyards where the carcases went from man to man along an overhead trolley, and each did a little bit of the work. When he had studied it and built an assembly line for his cars, he could make a car, from start to finish, in three minutes."

"Go on!"

"It true."

Artie got up and paced about, puffing furiously at his pipe, clearly excited at the implications. Then he stopped and looked around the yard, and the excitement escaped from him like water draining out of a ruptured bucket. His excitement turned to anger.

"What are you telling me all this for? It's no fucking use to me."

"Anything that makes you think is useful."

Artie knocked the ash out of his pipe, pulled out an enormous fob watch and stalked over to the clock to punch in.

"Smack!" he shouted. "Time to clock in."

***

The next few hours were spent in silence, but Curly was aware of the long glances that came his way from a tense Artie. But he had his own thoughts to contend with. He wondered how his beloved Buick would look if subjected to this level of engineering. There would be none of the sensual curves of the bodywork or none of the swoops of the chrome if they had been subjected to a forming process after the various levels of surface finishing had been carried out. His knowledge of engineering was very basic, but he would hazard a guess that to make anything with such a disregard for consequences would be to nullify any purpose in the making of things, any satisfaction of doing a job as well as it could be done. Even these damned sheets, destined as they were to be incorporated into some sort of holding structure and placed as they would be against the wall of some factory, or warehouse or office, deserved better.

His years of training at dance, his carefully-thought-out moves, rehearsed and rehearsed until his very bones knew them, had imbued in him a respect for doing everything he did as well as he could, even if those damned producers didn't recognise how difficult it had been to perform at what he knew was an international standard. Oops! This repetitive, boring bending process left too little to keep the mind busy and to stop a descent into maudlin self-pity. Poor, put-upon Curly Collins, unappreciated by a cruel, heart-hearted world and cast adrift into the slough of Ballymalloy. Smack came into sight as he pedalled past the shed and out into the street, and Curly laughed aloud at his own emotional wallowing. Bend. Bend. Bend until your bones crack. Until your heart breaks. Until your very soul shatters. He worked away at the press grinning wildly and causing Artie, who saw his contorted green face, to wonder if Curly had been driven mad by the paint fumes.

**

At lunchtime a few days later, Curly decided he wanted to take the Buick for a spin to experience again the feeling of power it imbued in him when he put it through its impressive paces; the silent surge when he stepped on the throttle and let the 170 horsepower loose, the way the huge four thousand pounds of bulk responded to the power steering, the envious glances of the townsfolk as he whispered past. As he came out into the main street, Smack on his delivery bike pedalled past him, glaring at Curly as if he dared to overtake his hurtling bicycle.

Joining in the fun of the moment, Curly hunched his shoulders and matched the Buick's speed to Smack's. They 'sped' along the main street side by side until Smack pulled across in front of him and stopped at the kerb, panting heavily but looking as David must have looked in the Valley of Elah. Curly stopped beside him and got out of the car, also panting. He walked over to Smack and held out his hand.

"It was a good race. I don't know the track as well as you, Smack. Congratulations."

Smack tentatively took the offered hand and was surprised and delighted at the vigour with which his hand was shook.

"Smack knows this place," he said, speaking more clearly than Curly had ever heard him speak.

"I know you do, and if ever I get to race this car in this town, I'll call for you as a co-driver. Now, come and see how the Buick handles." He turned towards the car and turned back again as Smack hesitated.

"Come on, Smack. You have to get to know this car."

He got into the Buick and opened the passenger door.

"Hop in. There's no time to lose."

Smack parked his bike and got in, delight and excitement written all over his face. For the first time, Curly felt he was dealing with a normal, excited adult. He started the Buick with a forward surge that threw Smack back in his seat. He sat up again, aglow with the wonder of this magical machine, the first motor car he had ever been inside. They accelerated down the main street with Smack clutching the dashboard and yelping in glee as Curly threw the car around a corner, throwing Smack against the door. Smack soon gained his upright seat and started to lean towards the car's centre.

"Bang!" he shouted. "Bang. Bang. Bang, bang, bang. Smack smacks back! Bang!"

Curly realised Smack was peering through the gun sight mascot on the front of the car and unleashing some imagined but devastating missile at the passing, or being passed, pedestrians as each filled the sight. The Buick drove along a few more streets and they annihilated several more enemies before returning to Smack's bike. When he stopped, Smack got out without a word and mounted his trusty steed. He turned and saluted at Curly, who saluted back, then he pedalled away. Strangely enough, Curly had a lump in his throat as he drove away.

***

Mary was putting glasses on a shelf in the hotel bar when Curly walked quietly in. He had scrubbed his face until it was raw, but strong traces of the dark green paint remained, except around his nose and face which had been covered by a stiff paper mask. He stood and watched her – and listened too – because she was singing in a pure, sweet voice:

"*With our swords and spears we gored them*
As through flood and tide we bore them
Ah, but Sean O Duibhir a Ghleanna
You were worsted in the game..."

She turned towards the bar and saw him.

"Mr Collins, you put the heart crossways in my chest."

"I'm sorry I startled you."

"Ah, it's my fault for being so highly strung. My mother used to say that I should be stretched across a fiddle. You look like a man who could use a pint."

"Now *that* is true."

She went to the dispenser and started to draw a pint.

"That song you were singing. It's all about death and killing."

"Most of the good songs are."

"A guy I met in a Dublin pub after a good old sing-song said a very interesting thing to me. He quoted some English poet who wrote:

The great Gaels of Ireland are the folks that God made mad.

'Cause all their wars are happy and all their songs are sad."

"He was right, there. Oh, hello, Mr Flannigan."

Freddie bustled in and crossed to Mary. He didn't see Curly sitting at the far end of the bar.

"I've been to the bank. They've given me money to renovate for the auditions."

Mary glanced in Curly's direction and Freddie turned and saw him.

"Oh, good afternoon, Mr Collins. I didn't see you there."

Mary carried on pouring the pint.

"It'll be a big event," Freddie carried on to Mary. "There'll be hundreds here. The papers, even the newsreel people. I'll redo the dining room too. Set it up for dinner dances."

"There'll be enough dancing for us all, but it'll be jive and jitterbug and even bop," said Mary. "What's bop like, Mr Collins?"

"I'll give you lessons sometime."

"*Can* you bop?"

"Oh yes. I can bop." He raised his glass. "Here's to bopping in Ballymalloy."

"I've ordered a new chiller for the beer," said Freddie. "The Dubliners like their beer cold."

"The cheek of them," Mary snorted. "They'll be wanting ice in July next. Why did they choose Ballymalloy, do you think?" she asked.

"One of the organisers said it was perfectly placed to cover Cork and Kerry," said Freddie. "They're having them in Killaloe to cover Clare and Tipperary. They're avoiding the cities. For some reason. They also want local dancers to audition. There has to be at least one couple who is local, or who has roots here, in each heat."

"Hell. You won't get anybody in this town who can dance to jazz," said Curly.

Freddie felt threatened.

"Oh yeah? What makes you so sure?"

"There you are, Mr Collins. Get outside of that," Mary said quickly, placing the pint in front of Curly.

"Thanks," Curly said, reaching for the drink awkwardly, trying to hide his fingernails. Her eyes dropped to them and she looked away quickly.

"What makes me so sure? Come on! Ballymalloy?"

"We have a proud dancing tradition in this neighbourhood, I'll have you know," replied Freddie. "We've produced many champions here."

"Yes. I've met one," said Curly. "Joy."

Mary was suddenly icy. "What about Joy?"

"Joy is a lovely and gracious woman but her style of dancing…?"

"There are other types of dancing here!"

"Like what? The waltz? The galop? The polka? The gavotte?"

"Well, Mr Collins," said Mary vehemently, "we have Irish dancing. With so many different styles and steps that they would make your head spin. Tap? We invented it. Long before you Yanks started to walk upright in your barn dances among the buffalo droppings."

In her anger, Curly thought he had never seen such flashing blue eyes – he had never noticed the colour of her eyes before – contrasted with a creamy skin with, at the moment, a bright pink flush over it.

"I could show you variations of the steps in an Irish jig that I would defy you to follow," said Mary, "and I could keep that up for as long as it would take you to sink that pint."

"I'm sorry, Mary. I know nothing about Irish dancing. I admit that. I have been so immersed in modern American dancing that I have not studied other forms of dancing. I know that all dancing styles all over the world are interconnected and that they evolve and grow from each other. I accept your correction and I apologise for my Yankee arrogance and ignorance."

They held each other's gaze for a long moment and Mary burst into a peal of laughter.

"Apologies accepted," she said with a grin. Curly bowed and this brought his face into the light cast over the bar by the bulb above.

"Lord, Mr Collins! What happened to your face? You look as if you were kissing an oyster."

"Spray painting. Between that and drilling millions of holes in mild steel a sixteenth of an inch thick, this factory has me destroyed."

"Spray painting?" asked Freddie.

"Spray painting," replied Curly.

"Dirty work that."

"Filthy work."

"Doesn't take much skill."

"You'd be surprised how difficult it is to apply it evenly."

"I'm sure I would."

"And not get any bubbles in it."

"I can well believe that."

"An American invention, spraying."

"Just like jazz."

"Will you two stop it!" said Mary. "Another pint, Mr Collins?"

"Thanks. I will."

"Dirty work," said Freddie as he checked the cash till.

"Vanishing cream," said Mary.

"What?'

"Vanishing cream will get rid of that paint. I'll let you have some."

"That's very kind of you. Can I come and collect it?'

"I'll leave it at reception. After all, we can't have you frightening our other guests, can we? There's your pint."

Baffled, he started on his pint. Mary turned away to tidy the shelves.

"Dirty work," said Freddie as he walked out.

The pale sunlight grew a little brighter as it swirled through Joy's snow-white hair. Mary was brushing it gently, enjoying its glow as the light passed through it.

"Your hair looks lovely."

Joy preened a bit. "Thanks, dear. The day I decided to stop dying it was a great test of my character, and a great liberation it was when I let go of vanity and found out that I had wasted so much energy on it. It was one of the many bad habits Joe led me into, dying my hair. When I grew the first strands of grey, I was quite pleased, thought it looked quite distinguished. But Joe wouldn't have it. My hair, all of it, had to be auburn, so I gave in. And you know what? When I got the first treatment, it wasn't at all like my natural auburn. It was somehow dead. Not real. It wasn't me. Wasn't mine. Then that same year, Joe started to go bald. He nearly died. Off he went to London to find the best wigmaker. And from then on, he never had a moment's peace. The wig was good, I'll say that, but it limited his life. One day, he was sitting in front of the fire without his wig, dozing, next to the little table there, with the same little crocheted cloth on it that I got from my mother, God rest her soul. In I breeze with Bridget, unexpected – and he was so taken aback that he grabbed the cloth and threw it over his head and the three of us sat there, having the cup of tea that she had asked for and Joe with this cloth over his head that nobody could mention or pretend to see. Served him right, making me change like that. A year after he died, I let my hair do what it wanted to do."

She looked at her white hair contentedly. "Now, I'm all me. Don't care. Take me or leave me. White hair and all."

She looked at Mary who was biting her lip.

"What's eating you?"

"I really can't go with you today."

"You have to. And it's your day off."

"Oh, Auntie Joy! Please don't make me."

"Mary, Mary, why so contrary?"

"He's been trying to get me into that car of his ever since he came here."

"Well, I don't blame him for that. Listen. I'll sit in the front and you'll sit in the back."

"I think many a girl's reputation ended in flitters in the back seat of that car."

"And her knickers too."

"Auntie Joy!"

"Well! What can he do with me around?"

"It's a picnic. And you'll have a glass of Amontillado—"

"Or two."

"Or two. And you'll doze off and I'll be left to his tender mercies."

"Mary, have you any idea how long it is since I had a picnic? The thought of a grassy slope with a strong man to push me around and carry me in and out of a splendid car, is something I really want to enjoy while I still have some time left to reflect on it afterwards. But it'll be a few hours and I'll need you to… help me do it."

"Oh, Auntie Joy. I'm sorry. I—"

A knock on the door interrupted.

"Hush *a leanbh*. There he is. Open the door. Don't forget the Amontillado."

***

Three hours later, in the Gap of Dunloe, Joy was dozing on a blanket and cushion on the springy grass amid the remains of a picnic lunch. The wheelchair lay on its side next to the blanket, and further up the slope Mary and Curly were strolling along the twisting roadway towards a viewing point above the lake. Mary stood on a huge weathered sandstone boulder and surveyed the road swinging down to a gushing stream that flowed out of the lake and out of sight around the curve of the variegated valley, which was a bowl holding the deep blue lake in its centre. The cumulous clouds were reflected in the waters as they drifted across from rim to rim. Some birds made their presence felt through gentle song, and from a huge clump of flowering shrub came the drowsy buzz of the bees about their work.

"Joy loves it here. And so do I." She stretched her arms out and let the breeze play with her hair. "I wish I could fly."

"Joy says it flushes out the brain cells."

"It does. So does a ride in that car. It's like flying, I imagine."

"How long has she been in the wheelchair?"

"Ages. It happened here."

"What did?"

"She fell."

"How?"

"She wouldn't tell. Some hikers found her and got her to hospital. She never spoke about it afterwards. It's one of the great mysteries of Ballymalloy."

Curly moved up beside her.

"You're another mystery. What is it about you that…"

She moved away lightly.

"The biggest mystery about me is why I'm still in Ballymalloy."

"You want to leave?"

"I want to go…" she pointed outward "…out there."

"That's the Atlantic Ocean."

"You know what I mean. Dublin."

"It's about an hour and a half along that road. In the Buick."

He moved closer again and she again retreated.

"What's out there for you, Mary MacBride?"

"I don't know. That's the beauty of it."

"It's a hard city for country girls; Dublin."

"Maybe, but Ballymalloy is so… predictable. There's no room for… dreams, I suppose."

"Dreams! Ha."

"You sound bitter."

"I am. I had a dream. Once."

"What happened?"

"I woke up."

"In Ballymalloy?"

He moved in for the kill. "There are worse places to wake up. And worse people to wake up beside."

She waited quietly until he put his arms around her waist and then gave him an unmerciful box on the ear.

"My, my," she said. "Another dream shattered."

7

The band

The hotel dining room had a partition running down the centre and the tables had been crammed together at one end. Freddie was trying to placate Mrs Smith who was having tea with her faithful spouse and feeling very disgruntled.

"It won't be for long," Freddie was saying. "You won't know the place when it's finished. It'll be bright and cheery and full of light music and happy people."

"That's what Smith is afraid of."

Mr Smith looked surprised at this.

"He needs his peace and quiet."

"Oh. Aah. Perhaps so," said the apple of her eye.

Freddie made his escape only to be stopped by Mary, who was holding a legal-looking paper.

"Mr Flannigan, you better read this."

Freddie grabbed the paper and walked into his tiny office behind the reception desk.

"They want a band," Mary said.

"A band! They'll have to supply their own."

"Not according to that contract."

"Where am I supposed to get a band in Ballymalloy? The last

band this place ever had was the awful police band that used to play every Sunday in the park."

He stopped and gazed into space.

"Get it."

"Mr Flannigan! The police band was disbanded years ago. Anyway, all they ever played were marches and the national anthem."

"No. They played some dance music too."

"But never jazz."

"Get them. They'll have to learn jazz. It's written down, isn't it? It must be. They'll have some in Dublin. Sort it out, Mary. I must look after the alterations."

He bustled out and Mary stood there nonplussed for a while.

"Policemen! I better go to the Garda station."

***

A few minutes' walk was all it took to reach the police station where Mary was soon seated with Garda Moriarty at his remarkably untidy desk. Their conversation was interrupted frequently by a drunk in the cell next door:

"Oh, the sons of the Prophet are brave men and bold
And quite unaccustomed to fear
But the bravest by far in the ranks of the Czar..."

Moriarty pounded on the wall.

"The ranks of the Shah, ye eejit! Of course we still play. He's been singing bits of the song for four hours and hasn't got any of it right yet. Didn't we play at the blessing of St Bride's Well last Sunday fortnight?"

The drunk started again:

"In the ranks of the Shah was Ivan Skavinsky Skevar..."

"Abdul Abulbul Amir! Get it right or I'll torture you!"

"And what sort of music do you play now?" Mary asked.

"All the songs and tunes that people round here like, and we're working our way through some grand Negro spirituals."

The drunk started again:

"One day the bould Abdul he shouldered his gun..."

"You can read music, though?"

"And donned his most truculent sneer.

Downtown he did go... downtown he did go..."

"I'll swing for that bowsie, as true as God!" Of course we can read. Anything."

"So you'll come to the hotel on Friday night?"

"We'll be there," Moriarty promised.

"And he trod on the foot... erm?"

Mary took her leave and headed back towards the hotel.

"On the toe. He trod on the toe, ye eejit!"

"Of Abdul Abulbul... no... Ivan Skavinsky Skevar."

***

That evening, when Mary was studying the telephone book behind the bar, Curly came in.

"Oh, good evening, Mr Collins. Pint?"

"Please. It's a dry and dusty job."

As she started to pour the drink, he eyed the directory.

"Looking for someone?"

"Yes. Someone who can sell me some music for jazz. For the auditions."

"Do you have a band to play it?"

"That I'm not sure of. The band I'm looking at has just discovered Negro spirituals."

"Then you'll need sheet music. Try Boosey and Hawks in Dublin."

"What sheet music should I ask for?"

"Let's see. Duke Ellington's *Take the A Train*. Billy Strayhorn's finest hour. Maybe a bit slow for auditions. *Opus One—*"

She placed the pint in front of him and grabbed a pencil and some paper.

"Wait. Wait. Slowly now."

"*Take the A Train,* Ellington. *Opus One* written by Sy Oliver for Tommy Dorsey. Miller's *American Patrol*, good, solid beat, not too fast. *Sing, Sing, Sing* arranged by Louie Prima for Benny Goodman. Oh. Let me think, there's more by Woody Herman, Count Basie, Artie Shaw. I'll have a good think after supper."

"You know them all?"

"Every riff. Every drum break. Every solo."

"Are you a musician?"

"No. Just a fan."

He took a good pull at the pint while she looked at him carefully.

"And it's all good music to dance to?"

"The best. Do you dance?"

"Oh, I've got medals for it. *Rince.* Irish dancing…"

She pulled back her shoulders, stretched her arms straight by her sides and danced some steps, surprisingly lightly.

"*Aon, do, tri. Aon, do, tri. Aon do tri cathar. Aon do tri.* I came first in *rince* at the *Feis Ceol* at the Puck Fair in Kilorglin. You've no idea what I'm talking about, have you?"

"Not a clue."

***

So, Curly made his list and Mary ordered the sheet music and it all arrived safely and speedily and was delivered to the police station, where it caused some considerable consternation among the members of the six-piece band comprising Moriarty as leader and pianist, a trumpet player, a clarinettist, a saxophonist, a bass player and a drummer.

That night, they had a first run-through of some of the pieces, and the consternation turned to something like panic, but Moriarty made them rehearse two of the pieces and, being experienced if not particularly talented, they found their way around the arrangements until they were dangerously close to smugness.

They were therefore, as ready as they could be for the first rehearsal in the hotel dining room in front of Freddie, Mary and Joy, who insisted on being there. Curly was in his room, sipping from a bottle of Irish whiskey and looking at the light fitting in the ceiling which cast a penumbra of shade over the corners of the room. He had considered taking a bath down the hall, but the thought of wrestling with the stiff taps, the thumping pipes and the difficulty of getting water that was somewhere between ice cold and scalding disinclined him. He lay, sipped and slipped into a half-doze.

Downstairs, Moriarty was working out which of the out-of-tune keys on the piano were to be avoided. He usually played the accordion, but it was totally out of character in a jazz band, so the old upright was the only option. He played a few tentative chords while the rest warmed their instruments up. The clarinettist was trying to set up his music stand without breaking another of his nails, and the drummer was quietly attacking the snare drum with a *very* strict tempo beat, more suitable for marching than swinging. Moriarty gave them a middle C and they all tried to repeat it. The he lifted his hand and they stopped blowing, strumming and tapping.

"Right," said Moriarty, arranging the sheet music. "*American Patrol*. Try to remember the drum break, John, and please let's have the clarinet and sax together for a change. One, two, one, two three and..."

They started. In terrible dissonance and very strict tempo. Freddie, Mary and Joy looked at them in stunned amazement. Upstairs, Curly was jerked upright by the din. It can't be? It's not possible! He covered his ears and looked at the box on top of the wardrobe. Downstairs, they laboured on, sweating and getting more and more discouraged, Freddie was about to vomit, Mary

75

was staring at the floor and Joy was getting madder and madder. The band came to the drum break and the drummer played it as if he was at a *ceili*; very wooden, very strict tempo and lacking all sense of swing.

Suddenly from the bar next door came the sound of *American Patrol* as Frank Meacham wrote it, Jerry Gray arranged it for swing and Glenn Miller played it. Moriarty shushed the band, which stopped raggedly, and they listened, awestruck. Into the dining room walked Curly with a record sleeve in one hand and the bottle of whiskey in the other. He nodded at Joy, put down the sleeve and whiskey and walked to Mary, holding out his hand to her. She blushed and stood up to face him. He moved backwards and accelerated evenly into a deft quickstep. She followed into his arms, going where he and the music led her. By surrendering her weight and momentum, she entered into that symbiotic relationship through which a good dancer can imbue a competent dancer with his or her skills.

Once they became a dancing couple rather than two individuals, they made good, even superlative, dancing look so easy. For the first few easily swinging but solid bars, they danced smoothly and well together until the build-up to the drum break happened. Right on the precise beat, he started to jive, suddenly pushing her hand away so that she was obliged to twirl around; when she faced him again, his hand was exactly in the right position so that hers had no option but to rest her fingers in his cupped ones and instinctively ready her supple body for another rhythmic revolution. So, he twirled her again and again, sometime with his catching hand behind his back, sometimes with their bodies so close together that they looked like one organism, sometimes with deft complicated moves with his feet as she soared at arm's length around him, skirt flaring, lovely legs twinkling. Those watching now understood how well-orchestrated swing music at a medium tempo could be the inspiration and the vehicle for a good-looking man and woman to shine on a dance floor. The band was equally inspired and discouraged. Joy had tears in her eyes; she kept loving eyes on her niece as Mary almost left the planet. When the snare drum ended its pounding break, Curly twirled her one more time, holding her hand loosely above her head, and stopped her as the band started to swing again. With a flourish, he deposited her back in her seat, glowing and exhilarated, bowed again to Joy, took up the sleeve and the whiskey and, placing the bottle on the piano, he left them all silent. Stopping the gramophone in the bar, he gathered it and the record up and made his way back to his room. God! Mary had the makings of a good, even a great, dancer, and she had looked so light and desirable as she twirled around him that he had felt his loins and mind stir at the thought of her in a much more intimate embrace.

***

Later that night, while Joy sipped her Amontillado nightcap, Mary was tidying up Joy's living room. She was dancing around the room, humming a reasonable imitation of *American Patrol*. Joy watched her as she sipped. Mary stopped humming and turned to Joy. She suddenly had on what Joy called her 'business face'.

"Now about your birthday party on Saturday, I've kept it small as you requested, just a few old friends—"

"I've invited a new one."

"Oh… you mean Curly."

"Yes. Have you changed your mind about him?"

"Oh, I still wouldn't trust him up a dark lane."

"And there's plenty of those in Ballymalloy."

Mary picked up a photograph of Joy and Joe and looked at it closely.

"Did you trust Uncle Joe?"

"Not as far as I could throw him."

"But you stayed with him for so long. Why?"

"Because he was a dancing man. Men are at their finest

when they're dancing. All that strength lightly borne. All their efforts aimed at making you look good. All their pride in their movements, their certainty as they throw you around. Dancing is what separates men from beasts. Makes them gods."

"That's sacrilegious, Auntie Joy."

"So what?"

"I'll tell Father O'Grady on you."

"See if I care. I wonder if *he* ever danced. Probably not. Too much of a temptation, I suppose."

"What did you think of tonight?'

"It was glorious. I know now why the world is going mad about jazz. The two of you were like angels. So light. So graceful. I wonder where he got the record."

"Oh, he brought a box of them with him. And a wind-up gramophone."

"Did he now? There's more to this Curly Collins than meets the eye. Where did he learn to dance like that? He has all the marks of a professional. What's he doing in Ballymalloy?"

"I think he's hiding from someone."

"Or something. From the law! He's a gangster!"

"Gangster my eye. Do you think he'd be spray painting at the factory if he was a gangster?"

"Well, he's hiding from something."

Mary wiped the photograph with her sleeve and placed it back precisely.

"Erm... how was I? At the dancing, I mean?'

"Like an angel." She took a sip and looked hard at Mary.

"Auntie Joy, I know that look. What are you plotting?"

"I think you should enter the auditions."

"Come on! Are you mad?"

There was no answer, just the steady stare.

"There'll be dancers from all over. I wouldn't stand a chance. Mary MacBride, a country girl!"

"That's what I was when Joe Murphy set eyes on me. He saw

the potential in me and drew it out. Took me over. That's what a good dancer can do. A man like him could make any woman look good. Like Curly Collins."

"If you think I'd let Curly Collins 'take me over', you have another think coming."

Joy said nothing. She finished her sherry and handed the glass to Mary who took it automatically. They were both silent as Joy wheeled herself towards the door and manoeuvred her way through it. As she went into the hall, she called out over her shoulder, "Come and settle me in when you've finished gawking at that photograph."

Mary didn't answer. She carried on gawking. Then she followed Joy along the hall and into the bathroom.

"Auntie Joy, have you any idea how much training you'd… I'd… need to compete at that level? And where would I get it?"

"Lots. And you'd get it from Curly."

She went into the bathroom and closed the door. Mary stood there, almost in shock. Learn from him? She did a little whirl. Well, why not? Her whirl had brought her in line with the mirror on the coat stand.

"What are you thinking, Mary MacBride?" she mouthed at her image, but as she moved into the kitchen to tidy up, she was still humming *American Patrol*.

***

Back in the dining room, the band were sitting in their allotted places, surrounded by a regimented array of whiskey bottles, the contents of which had been transferred to their stomachs with consummate ease. Moriarty was trying to play the supporting chords in the right rhythm. And failing.

"It must be in the genes." he said.

John the drummer was examining his sticks and the snare drum.

"I think it's in the elbows," he replied.

He started to wave his arms around loosely as the others looked at him blearily. John slouched over the drum and started to bang out the opening short rolls in straight rhythm as written, but at the indicated syncopated beat, he swung into the correct loose-elbowed beat that the part demanded. He played a few bars and looked at his sticks in amazement.

"Who turned them on?" he asked.

Moriarty sat up straighter.

"What did you just do?"

"I did this."

He played the section again. This time, it was longer and swung even more with a few grace beats he inserted. He stopped after a few bars and grinned at Moriarty.

Moriarty rested his hands lightly on the keys and gestured to the rest who took to their instruments.

"Do it again and keep it up. Right, lads? One, two, one, two three..."

It was better but not much.

"No! No!" said John, "it's in the elbows. Like this."

He waved his arms like a demented octopus. They all wiggled their shoulders and relaxed, made cocky by the whiskey, excited by the imminent possibility, and waited for Moriarty's count-in again. This time, it was much better. They finally got it. Strict tempo gave way to swing. Syncopation lurked in every bar, and the easy drive of the great arrangement finally made sense. A lot of sense. They played up to the drum break which John slid into easily and smoothly. When it was finished, Moriarty signalled a stop.

"It's playing at all them processions and hurling matches that has us ruined," said Moriarty, who picked up a whiskey bottle and kissed it.

"Me life on you," he said. "I hope we all remember all this tomorrow."

8

The confession

On Saturday morning, Mary was in the church for her monthly confession. She was early, so she was first in the pew; a fact that displeased Mrs Smith who, being second, took her place with all the dignity a really errant confessor should muster, as if her misdeeds were on such an exalted plane that common or garden sinners would be in considerable awe of her transgression if they but knew.

Her branch of the Smith family had bred a fascinating assortment of villains, and she had always thought of herself as having dangerous impulses inside her which, if let loose, would probably merit the various hangings, garrottings, shootings, beheadings and such punishments that had been inflicted on her ancestors and had thrilled her as a young girl. O'Grady understood her disappointment at the paltriness of her sins and had the sense to gratify her with some serious penances; ten decades of the rosary had elicited a satisfied sigh from her when administered; and the odd Nicean Creed, a grunt of satisfaction. Not for this paragon of incipient evil a mere three Hail Marys, thank you very much.

Her light o' love, Mr Smith, wondered, as he wondered every

Saturday, why on earth he should be again in this penitent's pew when sin hadn't darkened his brow, his thoughts or his conscience in many a turgid decade. He had long ago decided that he would use the seven deadly sins – all except lust of course – as a checklist to measure his behaviour against. This subterfuge had stopped his weekly confessions from being of acute embarrassment to himself and Father O'Grady. But he was a dim man, in appearance, in presence and in action, so the sins he confessed to bore a considerably diminished relationship to the actions, decreed by the Church Fathers many centuries ago, as those that offended God the most. Thus, shaving carefully every day became pride, not shaving became sloth, swearing mildly at Mrs Smith (under his breath of course) became anger, the desire to drive in Collins' Buick became covetousness, wanting to have a head of hair as luxurious as Collins' became envy, and taking another biscuit at tea, under Mrs Smith's disapproving gaze, became gluttony. So, without divulging the actual acts to O'Grady, he could announce in his confession as 'having committed the sin of pride'. O'Grady played along, never asked the details and dispensed the usual penance of three Hail Marys. So, face was saved every Saturday.

Father O'Grady came into the church, genuflected at the altar as he crossed the aisle, and entered the confessional, without a glance at the people awaiting him. Mary was hard upon his heels and was soon past the obligatory phrases and into her sins.

"Night after night, I have these amazing dreams about driving very, very fast."

"Well, there's nothing in the Catechism against fast driving."

"But I wake up in the morning very excited!"

"Hmmm."

"And I have immodest thoughts."

"Aah."

Mary flared up.

"And the sickening thing is that they're about a man that I don't even like."

"Still, an immodest thought is an immodest thought."

"Yes! So, you better give me a good penance."

"Oh, I'll give you the most severe penance allowed by canon law."

"Good."

"And if that isn't severe enough for you, I'll go back to the Inquisition. A good *auto de fe* would compensate for those immodest thoughts, and I might also take Ballymalloy's mind off the dancing contest."

"What's an *auto de fe*?"

"A burning at the stake."

"Ah, no. A few Hail Marys will do."

"Fair enough. A few Hail Marys it is."

Duly shriven, Mary hastened to Joy's house, where Minnie was laying the table for the birthday party.

"That looks grand, Minnie."

"Thanks. The cake'll be ready by now."

"We'll go and collect it."

Minnie fussed with the cutlery.

"A few of us were mentioning that fella."

"What fella?"

"You know very well what fella. The fella that has Ballymalloy by the ears. The buck in the Buick."

"Oh, him."

"Oh, him! I hear you danced with him the other night."

"Only for a minute or two."

"How did it happen?"

How it had happened was soon related. Minnie was all agog.

"What was it like? The dancing?"

Mary remembered and for a moment thought how good it had felt.

"Well?" Minnie had settled herself for a good old chat.

"The dancing was... amazing. I found myself doing steps and turns that I never even knew I knew. I suppose I didn't know them. It's just that, he made me do them. There wasn't room for any other steps. Those dances we used to go to, where they'd play the odd quickstep or foxtrot, it was nothing like that. It was like driving in that Buick and not in the old Ford rattletrap that Freddie owns."

"You've been in the Buick?"

"Yes. It's like floating, and I was floating in that dance. The only thing that kept me on the floor was his hand. Always there. In the right place. Making sense of the music."

Mary stared into space and Minnie stared at Mary.

"Girl. You've got to get him to teach you how to bop, jive, whatever it is."

"Are you mad? Step into those arms of my own free will?"

"You did the other night."

"That was… different. Anyway, it would get me into terrible trouble."

"Trouble or not, it would get you to Dublin."

They were dwelling on the implications when a scuffle was heard at the front door. Mary ran to open it and found Father O'Grady trying to manoeuvre Joy's wheelchair through. She ran to help and bent to kiss Joy.

"Let me, please. Father, it's good of you to take Auntie Joy home."

"No trouble at all. Where shall I deposit the lady?'

"In the lounge, Father. Auntie Joy, the cake is ready at O'Reilly's. Minnie and I are going to collect it."

"Hello, Father. Hello, Auntie Joy," said Minnie as she emerged from the lounge. "The table is ready."

The table was indeed ready and it looked very well.

"Oh, thank you both. It looks lovely."

"Are you staying, Father?" asked Mary.

"No, I'm not. I'm off directly."

"But you'll be back in time?"

"I will. O'Reilly's cake is like a siren."

Mary and Minnie departed, and Father O'Grady deposited Joy at her favourite station.

"Anything I can do before I go?'

"No, thanks." She paused. "Father, it's not fair to keep Mary here."

"It wouldn't be fair to you if she went. The fact of the matter is that you can't manage on your own."

"I can always sell this place and move into the hotel. There's so little for her to do in Ballymalloy."

"Except, I'm given to understand, to fend off the man in the Yankee chariot."

Joy rubbed her legs.

"Fending off men is a family weakness."

"Were you behind the door when they were handing out the fenders?"

"I was and I've been doing penance for it ever since."

"I'm not talking about your life with Joe, although that did merit a quantum of penance. I mean what you did – or tried to do – when he died. You've never confessed that."

"Confess what? I fell."

"That's the public version. But Joy de Burg, the most agile woman in West Cork, could never fall on such gentle slopes. What you did with Joe was bad enough, but what you intended to do was grievous. Your eternal soul—"

Joy suddenly flared up.

"Why do you have to bring this up on my birthday? Are you trying to spoil it?"

"Birthdays are good days for reflection on eternity."

"I've spent an eternity in this chair, Father. I'm not afraid of it anymore."

There was a standoff for a few moments, then Father O'Grady placed his hand gently on Joy's. She in turn placed her other hand on his.

"I do it for your own good," he said.

"I know. Don't be late coming back. You've never missed my birthday."

"Never. The cake calls."

He rose and left the room. The sound of the front door opening was accompanied by two male voices.

"Hello, Father."

"Ah, I'm just leaving. Joy's inside. I'll be back in a little while."

The front door closed and the lounge door opened to reveal Curly holding a small parcel.

"Hello, Curly. Thanks for coming."

He crossed the room and handed her the package.

"It was nice of you to ask me. Happy birthday."

Joy opened the package and took out a small silver trophy with a jiving couple on top. She read the inscription.

"My! You *were* good. Pour me a sherry; there's a good buccaneer."

She pushed herself over to the side table and placed the trophy next to the photograph of her and Joe.

"That's where you belong. Next to my Joe. He was quite… untrustworthy. Like all dancers."

She took the sherry with a nod of thanks.

"So, you *were* a professional dancer."

"I was."

"How did you get into it?"

"Through music. I got a trumpet when I was about eleven years of age. An uncle gave his to me when he got old and his breath let him down. I jumped in the deep end, tried to copy such players as Harry James and Bunny Berrigan, instead of buying a tutor and practising scales, so I didn't get very far. What I should have done was join the school band, but I thought the music it played was beneath me. On top of that, we lived in a block of flats in New York which was populated by cranky old men and women who couldn't bear my practising. So, to keep them happy, my mother told me to muffle the trumpet somehow. The only way I could do that was to kneel at the side of the bed, put the bell of the horn under the blankets and the printed tutor on a pillow. I blushed at the thought of Harry James seeing me like that, so I gave it up."

"And the dancing?"

"I was always pretty nifty on my feet and started copying Fred Astaire and Gene Kelly. I'd come home from the movies and work on the steps they did. I became pretty good too. Then I managed to get into a dancing school down the West Side, run by an old negro who could do some mean tap. I did well there and picked up more and more dance jobs in small theatres and clubs and then some good gigs in some shows off Broadway, I was even a stand-in for a Broadway show, which gave me three performances. Hell, that theatre, that audience, a great swing band and some pretty neat routines. I didn't eat much in those days but I danced a lot. Then…"

"Then?"

"I auditioned for the *Jazz* show. Didn't get past the first four bars." He was silent for a long while.

"That finished you? One rejection?"

"Yeah. Well, I was over thirty and the new dancers were… they were so fast and so strong." Another silence.

"So, you ran away to Ireland."

"Yeah. And the *Jazz* show followed me. All the way to Ballymalloy."

"Well, Curly, maybe you'll find a way to stop running here."

"Maybe."

Joy turned her chair around and indicated an ornate silver box on another side table, with a handle on the side.

"Wind that up," she said. "Gently. And when the handle starts to get stiff, stop winding and open the lid."

Curly did what he was told. It was a music box, and when the lid rose, the dulcet tones of *The Blue Danube* filled the room.

"Joe and I brought the waltz to Ballymalloy; can you believe that?"

She started to sway to the music, gently wafting her arms around. Curly stepped forward, took the sherry out of her hand and laid it on the table. He then took the arms of the wheelchair and started to waltz, pulling the chair forwards and pushing it back and moving it in a circle. Joy's swaying and graceful arm movements gave a faint indication of her grace as a dancer. Then Curly took Joy's hands and used them to gently spin the chair. She closed her eyes and gave herself over to the music.

"The whole town was scandalised that Saturday night as we swooped around the floor. I felt so wicked and Joe was grinning like a devil."

Holding one of her hands and an arm of the chair, he swung it in a circle around the clear space in the room.

"Oh, we shocked them out of their minuets and Sir Roger de Coverleys. My skirts were so full, those sitting in the front had to move their heads back. I was flicking my tail at them. The town gave me the silent treatment for a while but I knew that I had... what'll I say... stimulated them. Once they saw me talking to Father O'Grady afterwards, they knew at least that I hadn't been ex-communicated, so they all started to learn to waltz, and some of them were good, very good. But I didn't care; I'd set the bar – and the hem of my skirts – very high."

The music slowed to a melodious stop. Joy reached for the sherry and sipped it, smiling contentedly.

"You're very good, Curly."

"Not as good as I once thought I was."

"That's why you're here and not sashaying around America!"

It was a statement and not a question.

"That loss. That rejection," she said, "it must have hurt you dreadfully."

Curly was surprised – and yet he wasn't. This once beautiful dancer knew, more than most, the pain of denigration, of being tossed aside and rendered redundant.

"I ran away from loss," Joy said slowly, "and all I got was a greater loss. Maybe you've run far enough. You can't run away from yourself, no matter how fast you run. Or how far. I tried but it wasn't my time. My legs paid the price of my cowardice, so now they're punishing me. But you've still got your strength, your dancing skill. Why waste it?"

"It's been a long road for me, Joy."

"What do they say? It's a long road indeed that doesn't have a turning." She suddenly grinned wickedly. "Anyway, you've travelled it in comfort in that car of yours."

The front door slammed open and Mary and Minnie bustled into the front room. Mary was carrying a cake box, and with Minnie's help, she took out the cake and laid it on the table.

"There. O'Reilly's finest."

A knock on the door sent Minnie hurrying to open it, and moments later the room was full of bodies as Father O'Grady and Freddie came in, all bonhomie and well wishing. Each had a present for Joy which she took, opened and put on a side table, having exclaimed their generosity.

"Cut the cake," ordered O'Grady. "It's the only reason I'm here."

Joy wheeled herself closer to the table and took the knife that Mary offered, as Minnie dispensed the sherry and some bottles of stout.

"You must make a wish when you cut it," said Freddie.

"I wish…" said Joy as the knife slid into the marzipan, "… that Mary wins at the dance auditions and gets to Dublin."

"What put that mad idea into your head, Auntie Joy?"

"It's not that mad," said Minnie as she started serving the cake. "Do you know…" she said as she served Curly, "… that she won first prize at the Puck Fair in Kilorglin, in the *rince*."

"Yes. So I've heard. Thanks." Curly took the cake and glanced at Mary.

Mary blushed slightly but shook her head dismissively. O'Grady cut into the awkward pause.

"How's the renovation going, Freddie?"

"Slowly enough. It's hard work."

"Dirty work?" asked Curly innocently.

Freddie glared at him and O'Grady cut in again.

"What's with this jitter jiving? Is it decent at all?'

"It'll do no harm to your flock, Father."

"I'm not so sure. We had terrible trouble about the movements of bodies a while back. I'm talking about heavenly bodies and those two troublemakers, Copernicus and Galileo."

There was a puzzled silence in the room.

"Many happy returns, Auntie Joy," said Mary and they all joined in loudly. Joy took it all as her due and then spoke.

"Thank you, and here's to the new style of dancing. You've no need to worry, Father. Ballymalloy survived the waltz, the Charleston and the Lindy Hop. It will certainly survive jive and bop. Especially since it seems that nobody in the town can do it."

"And that's going to be a problem. According to the rules, there has to be a local dancer in the contest. Isn't that right, Mr Flannigan?"

"It is," Freddie replied, "but I rang an agent in Dublin and he's sending me two professional dancers just back from America. He says their people, at least his people, came from West Cork, so they qualify to represent Ballymalloy. They've danced on Broadway. A Darcy and Mitzi Power."

Mary was looking at Curly as he nearly choked on his sherry.

"Do you know them, Mr Collins?"

"I've… heard of them. They're supposed to be very good."

"Why would they bother to come here to enter the contest?"

"Because winning in Ballymalloy is a sure thing. No competition worth bothering about. It'll get them into the national finals."

"What sort of a name is Mitzi?" Minnie asked the room.

"It's a name you won't hear at the baptismal font in my church," said O'Grady. "Good health again, Joy."

They all toasted her again, Curly absently, which Mary noticed.

"Good health to us all," Joy repeated. "Mary, cut a piece of the cake for Smack."

Later, they all left as they went their various ways. Mary found herself being escorted back to the hotel by Curly and they walked along silently for a while. Then Mary stopped and faced him.

"Your dancing…"

"What?"

"You'll only get a swelled head."

"No," he said and paused. "I won't get that."

"Were you a professional dancer?"

Curly paused before replying.

"I was."

"What happened?"

"I… I got old."

Mary burst out laughing.

"It's true. You have a few years at the top and then the younger guys catch up with you. They're faster, they're stronger and they're braver. Not by much but enough to make a difference when it really matters. And the styles are changing fast right now. Like the jazz. It's all more demanding."

"If… a dancer got into that show in Dublin…"

"He – or she – would do well. Especially when it travels. To London, Paris, Berlin. Maybe even a reprise in New York after a couple of years. Yeah. They'd do well."

He stopped and looked at her.

"You want to know if you have the potential?"

"You've danced with me. What do you think?"

"It's hard to say after one, very short, dance. I'd have to do a proper assessment."

"And how would you do that?"

"I'd have to do a slow dance with you."

"Why am I not surprised?"

"Seriously. The slower the dance, the more control you need."

"Could you beat Darcy Power?"

"Yeah. Once."

They walked on, each wrapped in thought.

***

The large cell at the back of the police station was the handiest place for the band to practise. The only window in the cell faced out onto a silage pit in the corner of a rarely used field away from the town itself, so the only audience for the music were the rats and the occasional farm labourers who dragged the silage away to be fed to the animals. The fermentation smell in the immediate vicinity rendered the back cell less than salubrious, so it was occupied only by the (rare) serious criminals and of course the rehearsing band whose alcohol intake rendered them immune to any likely infections, apart from headaches, which they attributed to their copious imbibitions. This rehearsal was no different; they were all well on the way to being decidedly drunk, pissed, footless, rat-arsed/faced, fiddler's bitch, Brahms and Liszt, newt-coot-and skunk-like. They were surrounded by empty bottles and rumpled sheet music, but Moriarty was still in charge.

"Now, as far as I can ascertain – or remember – you become relaxed enough to play this jazz between the fifth and the eighth drink."

The trumpet player spoke up.

"And how many have we had?"

"Three," hazarded the saxophone player. "Or was it four?"

"Five," said the drummer. "But who's counting?"

"There's a long solo in here," said the trumpet player. "I'll never make it with these dentures. They're loose."

"You don't play with your teeth," said the clarinettist.

The trumpet player was indignant.

"My embou... embou... Christ, I can't say it."

"Your embouchure," supplied Moriarty.

"Yeah, thanks. My embouchure relies on my teeth, and mine are loose."

"Well, let's have a go," said Moriarty. "Now, John. JOHN!"

"What?" said the drummer.

This is *Sing Sing Sing*. And the drum has to swing, swing, swing. Okay?" He was pleased with this witticism, but they all looked at him owlishly. "Okay. One, two—"

"Abdul Abulbul Ameer" came screeching from the next cell.

"Shut up or I'll throw you out!" roared Moriarty.

"Out of jail?"

"To gobshites like him, it's the Ritz. Right, lads. One, two, one two three."

The drummer played the supposedly pounding intro in a leaden manner. The rest came in raggedly and Moriarty pulled at his scant hair.

"Stop! Stop!" he almost sobbed.

"Who's molesting them bagpipes in there?" came from the next cell.

"Another drink all round," said Moriarty. They obliged and he counted them in again. This time, the drummer did his octopus routine and the intro really swung. Moriarty shouted over it.

"Follow him. Follow him. And the devil take the hindmost."

They did and it wasn't that bad at all. The trumpet player had a raw, raucous sound that matched the mood of the piece. Right up to the first clarinet break, they all enjoyed themselves and exchanged enthusiastic nods with each other. Then the clarinet solo faded away to nothing. They all stopped and looked daggers at the clarinettist.

"I forgot to take a breath beforehand. Sorry."

"Well, that wasn't bad. We'll try that again. Rome wasn't built in a day."

"Wasn't it?" asked the trumpet player.

"Okay, from the top; one, two, one two three—"
"Oh the sons of the prophet were bold men and brave
And quite unaccustomed to fear
But the bravest by far in the ranks of the Czar—"
"The Shah! The Shah!" they all shouted.

9

The seduction

The Buick crept through the streets of Ballymalloy, like some bloated and wickedly grinning alien. The few street lamps winked on the chrome grill, imbuing it with menace, and slid over the shiny bodywork furtively as if trying to break up its bulk into dimly seen curves and shadows. The headlights were switched off, and it was as if a dangerous behemoth was on the hunt for lost souls and tender bodies. It passed the black railings around the church while Father O'Grady was walking slowly past the graveyard. He stopped as the sullen Stygian shape whispered by, and crossed himself with a shiver. The car moved on and turned into the side street where Joy's cottage stood. It stopped a little beyond it in the umbra of a well-leafed tree.

The door of the Buick opened and Curly stepped out, carrying a single record. He surveyed the cottage, noting the light in the living room and a very dim light in the window on the opposite side, which he knew was Joy's bedroom. Moving to the living room window, he tapped a soft rhythmic riff on the glass. When the curtains opened, he held up the record so that Mary could see it. She stood a while in thought and then moved towards the hallway and the front door. Curly moved to the door, and when it opened, he stepped through and held the record out as if it were a peace offering. Mary returned to the living room with Curly on her heels. Joy's head appeared in the window of her room as she looked out and then moved back. Mary stood in the centre of the living room as Curly went to the ornate gramophone, placed the record on the turntable and wound up the machine. He lowered the volume and placed the stylus on the shellac. The soft strains of Glenn Miller's *Moonlight Serenade* filled the darkly lit room as Curly stepped towards Mary and held out his arms.

"Let's see how good you are," he whispered.

"In what sense?"

"As a dancer, of course."

"Of course."

She moved into his arms and he held her gently.

"Go with the music. Keep your thigh pressed against mine and do as I do. You'll know which way I'm going to go."

As the woodwinds, with clarinet leading, started the theme, with the brass gently interjecting, she became caught up in the music, the dancing and, she – grudgingly – accepted, the man and moved with him, gaining confidence and losing inhibitions as she did so.

"That's better," he whispered in her ear.

"Is this your secret weapon?"

"Shh! Go where the music tells you."

He edged towards the door, turned the handle and pulled it open.

"The music is telling me nothing about the hallway." She breathed and pushed the door closed.

In time with the slow and relaxed melody, the door was pulled open, pushed closed and, as it got wider, he kissed her, softly at first and then with increasing urgency. Inexorably, they were out in the hallway.

"Which is your room?" he asked. She stopped and looked

at him for a few sensuous bars and then turned to her doorway and opened it. Curly closed the living room door and followed her, but she stepped through the doorway and closed the door behind her. He heard the key turn in the lock and tried the handle but it wouldn't budge. With a short, sharp intake of breath, he returned to the living room and crossed to the gramophone. Moments later, he stepped out through the front door, record in hand, and crossed to the Buick. As he got in, Joy's shadow moved across the window and stopped as she looked out. The Buick pulled away with a gentle spray of dust and Joy moved back into her room.

***

The hotel hadn't seen such bustle and confusion since its construction one hundred and twenty years previously. Mrs Smith had insisted on their usual table next to the window and there she and her consort sat, she resolutely ignoring the passing workmen and he cowering as each ladder or beam of wood passed perilously close to their heads. She was deaf to the cacophony of whistles, shouts and orders that whirled around them; noises that, since the emergence of physical labour as a means of earning a living, had been deemed essential for the completion of any job. He, however, winced as each shrill sound rattled around them. Mary approached, carrying a laden tea tray, and started to serve them.

"Nice to see you back in your usual place, Mrs Smith – and Mr Smith." she said over the din.

"Nice to see you looking particularly well, my dear," Mr Smith hazarded.

Mrs Smith looked disgusted, Mary looked guilty and Mr Smith looked contrite. As Mary turned away in some embarrassment, she came close to colliding with an earnest-looking man in very hairy tweed with a cigarette hanging from a pendulous mouth, exuding a column of ash longer than she had ever seen. Behind him came a scrawny youth carrying a bulky wire recorder slung around his long, lumpy neck.

"Can I help you?" she asked. "I work here."

"Really? Yes, you can. I'm from Radio Eireann. I'm here to cover the dance auditions. For broadcast."

"Dancing? On radio?"

"Oh, I'm not really interested in the dancing *per se*. I'm really interested in the psychology and, I daresay, the cultural impact of such auditions on a small town in…"

"West Cork," she volunteered.

"Exactly! That's what I'm *really* interested in." The stress on the last 'really' dislodged the column of ash, somewhat to Mary's disappointment, but a couple of deep inhalations started a new column as the first dispersed itself over the ample expanse of hairy tweed.

"Really?" she ventured. "Then you'll want to talk to my boss, Mr Flannigan. He's the one who brought the dancing to Ballymalloy."

"Really? Is he here?"

"Rea… yes. He's here. I'll fetch him."

She dodged around the scrawny youth, who was waving a microphone around vaguely, and hurried into the bar. There she found Freddie serving behind the bar, and Curly was in his usual corner, talking intently to Minnie. Mary looked suspiciously at them, blushed and turned to Freddie.

"Mr Flannigan. A man from Radio Eireann is here. He wants to broadcast the dance auditions."

"Dancing? On radio?"

"Not the dancing. The… cultural impact."

"Really?"

"I wouldn't use that word with him."

Freddie rushed out and Mary moved down to where Curly and Minnie were sitting, nursing drinks.

"Hello, Minnie." She turned to Curly as Minnie murmured a hello. "I haven't seen you around lately, Mr Collins."

"I've been to Dublin for a couple of days."

"Dublin! Why?"

"To pick up a spare tyre for the Buick."

"Oh. When… I mean, are we… going to…?"

"Let's go for a drive this evening."

A customer burst into the bar.

"Hey, Mary. I'm dying for a pint."

"Coming," she called out. "I'll see you later then."

She started to draw the pint. Curly finished his drink and muttered a goodbye to Minnie. As he passed Mary, they exchanged glances and nods. As she worked on the pint, she looked towards Minnie and saw that she was looking after Curly. The two girls looked at each other and Minnie looked down at her drink. Mary served the customer his pint and left the bar. She hurried to Freddie's office to find him poring over some documents.

"How was it?" she asked.

"*Really* interesting. Seriously, it's going to be valuable publicity."

"I'm glad. Well, if you have no further need of me, I'll—"

"Sit a moment, please."

Mary sat but on the edge of her chair. She had a premonition that what Freddie was going to say would be serious. Or was she projecting her inner turmoil onto the most mundane events and remarks?

"Mary, I'm pretty sure these dance auditions are going to put the hotel back on its feet." He grinned. "I'm *really* sure. If… when… it does, I won't be able to handle all the extra business on my own, and anyway, I will have to concentrate on building on this event in various markets. So…"

Mary was on tenterhooks as he paused and looked hard at her.

"So…" Freddie continued, "I want – would like – you to be my assistant manager."

She sat and was silent.

"What do you say, Mary?"

"I… I need time to think about it. I… might even be moving to Dublin. I don't know. Thank you, Mr Flannigan, for the thought. I… I just need time."

There was a long pause before he spoke.

"Mary, are you sure about what… what's happening? What you're doing? Or going to do?"

"No. No, I'm not."

"There are some men who…"

"I know."

There was a long silence before she rose to her feet and made for the door where she turned to face him.

"It's very kind of you, Mr Flannigan," she said before she turned and went out.

***

This time, the Buick was acting like a drunken black whale. It surged, lurched and swerved from side to side on the gravel road, spraying a wake of dust, grit and shrieks as it made its erratic way through the Gap of Dunloe, threatening the rudimentary rock barrier that tried to retain the road's essential shape and direction. An oncoming donkey and trap was forced to scrabble frantically up a side slope as the donkey-eating beast came growling along. The language of the trap driver stretched the blasphemous capabilities of the English language to its linguistic limits as the enormous car passed by, and the airy wave from Curly only elicited a fresh vomit of abuse which would have demonstrated to him the limitless source of obscenity which an uneducated countryman can summon up at a moment's notice, especially when that moment seems to be the last granted him in the land of the living.

"Take it easy," said Curly to a very nervous Mary who was

wrestling with the enormous steering wheel. "Driving is just a matter of getting the right response – out of the engine. Especially this engine. It's a straight eight."

"What on earth – oops! – is a straight eight?"

"Eight cylinders all in a line. Don't struggle with the wheel. Just let the car right itself. Yes. Like that. See? Don't fight it. Go with the flow – the Dynaflow. Yeehaw!"

"Don't yell like that. I'm trying to concentrate."

Strangely enough, when she did let the car's momentum and sensitive power steering do what it was designed to do, the driving became easier and she started to enjoy the sense of power the Buick imbued in her.

"See?" he said, "a car is like a woman."

"You've got a nerve!"

"I'm serious. You can't use force with either."

She cast as much of a glance at him as the driving allowed.

"Well, you'd know about that, wouldn't you?"

"Now, don't be cruel."

There was a short silence and he noted that the next glance was softer.

"You're doing fine now," he said. "Jesus!"

The last ejaculation was in response to an off-road swerve which she barely controlled. She braked hard and he hurriedly put on the handbrake. They sat there in silence looking at the cloud-dappled water of the lake.

"That was fun," Mary said contentedly. She looked along the road northwards. "An hour to Dublin, you say? Let's go. We could be there before dark."

He reached out and stroked her hair.

"The Buick has got you all revved up," he said softly.

"I know. It's a grand feeling. Let's go."

"Let's stay here for a while."

They looked at each other for a long time before he leaned forward and kissed her as she had never been kissed before.

This wasn't a grabbed kiss, a hurried collision of mouths, a brief exchange of usually not-so-fragrant breaths in the dark in a faint miasma of perspiration after a highly energetic dance. This was a lingering exploration of her lips and tongue by a man who wanted to know and experience all her secret places. His hands too knew exactly what they were about; her soft swellings, undulating curves and gentle swoopings.

"Get in the back," he breathed into her open mouth.

She giggled without moving her lips away.

"No. I'd rather stay here in the front with you."

He laughed too, got out of the car and stood waiting with his hands held out as he had held them out at their first dance together. She took a deep breath and got out, moving towards the back door. He opened it and she slid in across the smooth and capacious seat. He followed and the door closed with a soft click.

Their lovemaking was soft first and then urgent. Their limbs entwined themselves together without any straining or obvious effort, and they consummated their mutual desire with a gentle inevitability. She gave herself to him openly and trustingly and wondered at his loss of self in the final thrusting while she felt his warmth and effusions wash through her body in a gentle benison. She had never felt so complete as she held him closely while he recovered himself and looked deep into her eyes with a soft pride.

When they awoke, they awoke together. It was dark and the clouds were scudding across the half-moon.

"It's the same old moon," she said with surprise.

"Why should it change?"

"Everything should change." She sat up and poked him in the ribs. "You, Mr Curly Collins, have undone years of work by the nuns and by Father O'Grady. I hope you're proud of yourself."

"Oh, I am."

"They'll all know."

"Who?"

"Every ould biddy in Ballymalloy. They'll see I'm different."

She threw herself back on top of him. "I'll have to leave the town in disgrace. Take me to Dublin, Curly."

He pulled away and rearranged his clothes. Soon he was the usual cool, detached, rather intimidating American and not the vulnerable lover she had just given her all to.

"Dublin! What's in Dublin for you?" he wanted to know.

"Everything that isn't in Ballymalloy. Why did you leave there?"

"Things didn't work out."

"What things?"

"Things! Jesus!"

He got out of the car and she moved to the door.

"I'm interested, Curly. Especially after... this. And especially about your life in Dublin."

Curly got back in the front seat and started the car. She closed the rear door softly and looked up at the moon. He started the engine.

"Dublin! Jesus!" he said harshly.

She looked at the moon.

"Dublin," she said softly.

10

The repentance

In the back cell in the police station, the band was well into rehearsal and making a fair interpretation of *In the Mood* The inebriation was getting less as their confidence grew, and Moriarty was hopeful that competence would win the race with delirium tremens. As they were coming to the first of the two four-bar breaks of silence towards the end, the Radio Eireann reporter and his soundman came in. At the break, he thought the silence was a polite pause for his entrance and he began to speak.

"Ah, good day, gentlemen, I—"

The music continued until it came to the second break. Again, the reporter thought it was for him.

"It's wonderful to hear the band for the—"

The music continued until the end with its rising final few bars, and Moriarty signalled a stop. This time, the reporter was unsure as to whether he should speak, so he remained silent. Moriarty broke the embarrassed silence.

"Can I help you?"

"Ah yes. Thank you. I'm really impressed that a band could be found in…"

"Ballymalloy."

"Exactly! I'm from Radio Eireann and I'm here to record the impact these dance auditions are having on the town. Do you mind if I record our conversation and perhaps some of your music?"

"No, we don't mind. Do we?"

The rest of the band shook their heads and then they all watched as the scrawny youth started to set up his cumbersome recorder and microphone on its stand. None of them had ever seen such advanced technology before, but by the time the column of ash had fallen on the hairy tweed, he was ready. And the youth started the recorder.

"Testing, one, two, three, four. Testing, one, two, three, four," he bellowed into the microphone and then stopped and reversed the wire.

"TESTING, ONE, TWO, THREE, FOUR. TESTING, ONE, TWO, THREE, FOUR," bellowed the recorder and they all winced. The youth placed the microphone close to Moriarty and said:

"On three."

He silently counted three with an emphatic hand but the hairy jacket spoke into the microphone.

"I'm with the band that will perform at the dance auditions in… Ballymalloy as they rehearse in their… plush rehearsal room in the…. erm… local police station, because the acoustics are the best in town." He turned to Moriarty.

Tell me, Mr… Moriarty--"

"Sergeant Moriarty."

"…Sergeant Moriarty, the leader of the band, what is the appellation by which this ensemble will be designated?"

"What?"

"The name of your band?"

"Well, we are known at every social and official gathering in Ballymalloy as the Ballymalloy Strict Tempo Semiquavers."

"Really?"

"Really. But for this occasion, we think we should have a more modern name."

"And that is?"

Moriarty sat a little straighter in his chair.

"Well, we are toying with the name Duke Moriarty and His Modern Men."

"No. We're not. Not us. Ha!" came from the band, and there was an embarrassed pause which the reporter broke.

"That's… really interesting. Perhaps we could hear one of the pieces of music you will play at the auditions?"

"Oh, we're not ready yet."

"And when will you be ready?"

"Shortly, shortly." At his signal, the bottle made its rounds and the scrawny youth gave instructions in a thin, squeaky voice.

"Could yiz all sit in a semicircle around the mic?"

They obliged noisily while the hairy tweed consulted his notes. As they set up, the scrawny youth was surreptitiously passed the bottle several times until his thin, rather damp nose grew a bright red. When they were all in place and each had played a few bars for the sake of the microphone, the scrawny youth indicated his readiness to the reporter. Moriarty counted them in – silently on the instructions of the scrawny youth – and they played a reasonable version of *In the Mood* until the reporter indicated enough. Moriarty thought, for the first time, that they had a chance of not being lynched for their swing music.

***

Later that night, Mary was in the hotel office on the phone with a schedule spread out before her. The office was dark except for a small desk lamp.

"So, those dates are fine. To confirm; there will be four judges and two officials, right? We confirm we have very comfortable accommodation for them. The venue has been redecorated and it looks splendid. What? The band?"

She crossed her fingers.

"The band is fine. Very good and up to date on modern music, jazz, swing, bop. Very good. I think that's it. The whole town is excited. Well, see you soon. Goodbye."

She hung up, folded the schedule, switched off the light and sat there in the darkness.

"Dublin," she whispered.

As she got to her feet and crossed to the door, there was the sound of a fumbling key at the front door. It opened and Curly staggered into reception. He turned to the door, his fingers on his lips and held out both hands. Minnie appeared from the darkness and stepped into them as he softly hummed *Moonlight Serenade*.

"You don't want to go to Dublin, do you?" he whispered.

"No. Just your room," Minnie whispered back.

"And you can't dance, can you?"

"Not a step."

"And you don't think you sit on the Holy Roman and Apostolic Holy Grail, do you?"

"No. Just me arse."

"That's my girl."

They both staggered up the stairs and Mary stood in the dark. In shock.

*

In most people's lives, a certain day of the week is indicative of the inexorable passage of time. For those who work for a salary or a wage, Monday is the day when loins must be girded and weekend casualness replaced by commercial obedience, if not resolve. For those who dislike their commercial labours, Friday is the day that has a whiff of weekend freedom; gears change, efforts slacken and expectations rise. For the truly devout, Sunday is a day of contemplation and resolve, for which the Church has devised several practices, duties and rituals, attendance at which is encouraged and absence frowned upon. For those who look to the Church for succour, Saturday is a day of deep reflection and confession of misdemeanours, large and small.

So, on the next Saturday morning, the church had many visitors, among who were those redoubtable pillars of pious obedience, Mr and Mrs Smith. They were sitting in the back row, close to the pew for confession, ready to move in when the time seemed appropriate, not so early as to generate gimlet-eyed suspicion, not so laggardly as to hint at lack of respect. She was watching the movements of bodies around the building. He was silently counting the uprights in the altar rail for the umpteenth time. Mrs Smith's eye was caught by the sight of Mary at the small shrine to the Virgin in the relative darkness of the rather skimpy ambulatory. She was inserting a small lit candle into a brass holder with trembling hands and her shoulders were shaking. Sensing some struggle of conscience, Mrs Smith nudged Mr Smith viciously in the ribs. He winced and lost count. She indicated Mary. He shook his head impatiently and started a recount.

Father O'Grady came out of the sacristy, genuflected in front of the altar and crossed to the confessional. Mary moved to the confessional pew and Mrs Smith jabbed Mr Smith and rushed to be in the pew next to Mary. Shaking his head in frustration, Mr Smith followed and took his dutiful place at his spouse's side. Mary rose and entered the side cubicle of the confessional and Mrs Smith grabbed Mr Smith's wrist and twisted it to take note of the time on his wristwatch. Mr Smith sighed, rubbed his wrist and put his eyes out of focus lest some other architectural feature demanded counting.

Inside the confessional, Father O'Grady slid back the grid.

"God bless you, my child."

"Bless me again, Father, oh, do." Mary started to sob.

"Bless you again, my child. And again."

"I have sinned."

Father O'Grady waited until Mary had controlled her sobs.

"I had… I committed immodest actions – *I had sex with a man!*" This in a vicious whisper.

"I see."

"I'm so ashamed."

"Ashamed at what you did or who you did it with?"

"Father!"

"I'm trying to work out your degree of repentance, my child."

"Oh, I repent all right. Now that…"

"Now that what?"

"Now that I know how little it meant to him."

"So, it wasn't worth putting your immortal soul in jeopardy?"

"No! No, it wasn't!"

This was so loud that Mrs Smith heard it and rammed a bony elbow into Mr Smith again. He muttered an imprecation under his breath and moved away from her. Inside the confessional, Father O'Grady looked heavenward for guidance and spoke gently.

"I know you're a good girl and a good Catholic, and I don't have to tell you that you gave away the greatest gift you have in your power to bestow."

"I know that… now."

"The saddest thing is, it seems to have been wasted. So, I'll let you decide on your own penance. I know it will be harsher than mine."

"Yes. It will be." She paused for a while. "But the penance shouldn't be all mine."

"Perhaps it won't. But that's not for you to decide. This is *your* confession. Now say an act of contrition."

She did, in a sobbing and trembling voice, while the priest wept inwardly for her pain.

Moments later, Mary emerged from the confessional, went straight to the altar rail and knelt down. Mrs Smith grabbed Mr

Smith's wrist again, and he almost howled as she twisted it to see the time. She nodded grimly.

"Ahem!" came from the confessional. Mrs Smith pushed her better half towards the confessional. She wanted to watch Mary.

11

The penance

The dining room was beginning to shape up. The main alterations were completed and all that remained was the painting and the new drapes that Freddie had splashed out on. Mr and Mrs Smith were at their usual table. A full plate of soup stood in front of a grim Mrs Smith while Mr Smith was finishing his with obvious enjoyment. Freddie passed by and was called imperiously to the table by Mrs Smith. He looked at the full soup plate in surprise.

"You didn't like your soup, Mrs Smith?"

"It was the way it was served."

"Sorry? What?"

"Mary banged it down. Smith got the fright of his life. He doesn't like his soup bruised."

Freddie took both plates away, exchanging a surprised look with Mr Smith. On the way to the kitchen, he passed a distraught and harassed Mary who was standing looking out of the window at nothing.

"Mrs Smith says you bruised the soup."

"I'll bruise a part of her that never saw soup," she rejoined.

Shortly afterwards, Mary came in carrying two full soup

plates. She hesitated as she passed Curly's empty table, and Mrs Smith noticed it.

"Not got her mind on the job," she said.

"Not looking her usual blooming self," Mr Smith ventured – and wished he hadn't.

"I'd say the bloom has gone." she said and then suddenly flared up at her swain. "Since when have you been looking at the bloom on a young woman?"

Mary arrived at the table and placed one plate with exaggerated slow motion in front of Mrs Smith and a fresh plate gently in front of Mr Smith, catching his sympathetic smile.

"We're running a bit late today and you were early." Mary managed to say with some politeness.

"Well, some of us don't have to spend as much time as others in confession," said Mrs Smith grimly. Mary was thunderstruck and had to choke off a shocked answer. She ran from the dining room, brushing past a surprised Freddie.

"Are you all right?" he asked.

"Yes. No. I have a splitting headache. The food is making me feel sick."

"Go home. We'll manage. Get some rest. Okay?"

"Okay." She rushed on towards the front door.

Walking back along the main street, Mary had an attack of small-town claustrophobia. Every twitch of every lace curtain of every window along her route made her feel as if every inhabitant of Ballymalloy knew of her slip, her moment of weakness, her shame, her folly at falling for an American with a big car, a big ego and a big appetite for women – any woman, as long as she would... she blushed again at what she had done with him. In a car! Like any... the word 'whore' flashed through her mind, but she couldn't think of that word and not reject it violently. She was a good, clean country girl who had made a mistake. A big mistake. Oh God! What if – no, she rejected the possibility of falling pregnant. That would be the end.

With such tormenting thoughts whirring in her head, she made for Joy's cottage.

Inside Joy's cottage, Joy was rearranging the photographs on her side tables.

"Right. Let's see if I can get all you ghosts in some sort of order." She started to sing in a thin, pure soprano.

"*Believe me if all those endearing young charms*
That I gaze on so fondly today..."

She picked up a photograph of herself and Joe Murphy and wiped it carefully.

"*Were to change by tomorrow and fleet in my arms*
Like fairy gifts fading away.'

"Ah, Tom Moore, your songs were for all of us, for all time."

She held the photograph to the light and looked at it lovingly.

"And you, Joe Murphy, what trouble you brought me – and happiness too."

The front door slammed open and Joy placed the photograph on her lap and wheeled herself into the hallway to see Mary, white and dishevelled, heading for her room.

"Mary! Who so early?"

"My head is splitting."

"Can I make you something?"

"No. No thanks, Auntie Joy."

"Have you eaten anything since breakfast? Hunger is a sure way to—"

"No. I mean I'm not hungry."

"I've been worried about you."

"I'm worried about me too."

"Why don't you talk about it?"

"To you?"

"Yes. To me."

"You wouldn't understand. What would you know about men anyway?"

Mary stopped, shocked and angry with herself for being so insensitive. She burst into tears, ran into her room and slammed the door behind her. Joy picked up the photograph and looked at it again. She started to sing *sotto voce* as she wheeled herself back into the living room.

"'And around the dear ruin, each wish of my heart
Would entwine itself verdantly still.'
What would I know?" she asked herself.

***

Curly had decided to give the factory a miss, maybe even leave it altogether. After all, what was there for him in Ballymalloy, now that...? His mind was buzzing; images of the two young women flickered through his consciousness like an old silent movie. He was conflicted about them; one all tenderness and sweet surrender, the other all physical energy and rumbustiousness. His reaction too was conflicted; gentle, almost reverent with one, sweaty endeavour and anxious urgency with the other. In an effort to stop those dark thoughts, he walked briskly down the main street and paused as he came to the church graveyard. *Lucky dead,* he thought, *far beyond all such conflicts.* If there *was* an afterlife, it sure wouldn't concern itself with his problems. His sins maybe, but not his problems. He turned in through the gate and started to stroll among the stones, idly scanning the inscriptions. His eye caught a movement behind one of the stones. It was Father O'Grady who was weeding an overgrown grave. The priest looked up and saw him.

"The very man. Give us a hand here, will you?"

Curly approached and caught a glimpse of the stone. It had the name 'O'Grady' inscribed on it.

"Is this...?"

"My father and mother."

114

Curly crouched down and started to pull out the weeds. Father O'Grady relaxed a bit and looked at him.

"A colleague of mine tells me there was a Buick like yours in Galway a month or two ago."

"It was mine."

"You get around a bit, so?"

"I suppose I do."

"You've left your tyre tracks – as it were – on many a… *boreen* in Ireland. Have you seen much of the country?"

"A good bit."

"How fast can that car go?"

"They advise you not to open the window above a speed of a hundred miles an hour."

"Go on! I wonder if man should ever travel that fast?"

There was a pause as Father O'Grady contemplated what he knew of this man and what he was permitted to say to him, considering the confidentiality of confession.

"Have you heard about the Brehons at all?" he finally asked.

Curly shrugged in a sort of 'I guess so' way.

"They were the judges who ruled Ireland for a long time from about two thousand years ago. They moved the law away from retaliation to compensation. Made it a civil rather than a criminal sort of process. Up until then, the principle of 'an eye for an eye' was common, but the Brehons cared more about the good of the community."

Curly had some indication as to where this was going but he listened in silence.

"So, they gave the evil doers an opportunity to redeem themselves by paying a fine or serving the community in some way, and everybody was better off."

Father O'Grady rose to his feet and surveyed the grave. "There. That's better. You know, an unhappy, wounded girl is no use to Ballymalloy, but a pure, happy girl, healed in spirit, is a great thing to see swinging down the main street. The

Brehons would approve of that. Good day to you, Mr Collins."

He moved away and left Curly sitting there, clutching a handful of weeds.

***

That afternoon, in the hotel yard, Curly was washing the Buick with a chamois and pail full of soapy water. He came to a stubborn piece of grease on the fender and rubbed it hard for a moment before wiping the soap off. Reflected in the bodywork was Joy's face, and the expression on her face wasn't pleasant.

"Pity you can't wipe away the harm you've done," Joy said. With a splash of suds, Curly washed her reflection away, but she changed position until her reflection appeared again.

"Have you any idea, Mr High and Mighty, what it means for a young girl like her to give up her virginity?"

He splashed again but she appeared further down.

"Am I embarrassing you? Good."

Another splash. Another image.

"You dancers are all the same. You lead with your middle leg."

Curly threw the bucket of water over the car, but it didn't wipe her image – or her words – out.

"She won't come out of her room. Freddie's very understanding, but he won't keep paying her if she doesn't work. What'll become of us now that you have had your moment of shabby pleasure?" She wheeled herself away, calling out over her shoulder, "We'll all be out on our arses, young man."

This time, Curly tried to wipe out his own reflection. Joy called out from the entrance into the street, "Out on our arses!"

Father O'Grady was passing and was brought up short by this outburst.

"You look as if you lost a salmon and caught a pinkeen," he said to her.

"I've given up on men."

"I'm not allowed to give up. Having faith in the Lord is easier and you're not so prone to disillusionment."

"The last thing I need now is a sermon. My God, men haven't changed."

"Not since Eve."

"And what in the name of all that's holy, would you know about Eve?" She came as close to a snarl as she was capable of as she wheeled away.

"What would I know indeed?" said Father O'Grady as he watched her move down the street.

***

Back in the hotel yard, Curly gave the Buick a final buffing, got into the car and started driving towards the gate but had to come to a screeching halt because Freddie was standing in the gateway, holding a length of metal pipe in his hand. The two men looked at each other for several seconds. Then Freddie raised the pipe and brought it down squarely on the gun-sight hood ornament. It and part of the bodywork around it crumpled under the blow. Swearing, Curly got out of the car and approached Freddie, who raised the pipe over his head, thought better of it and lurched towards Curly, drawing back his arm for a hefty punch to the face. Curly swayed gracefully out of the way and stood poised on the balls of his feet. Freddie swung again. Another sway and another miss. A third powerful swing had Curly dancing away, his hands at his sides, and Freddie almost lost his footing. He stood there, panting and red-faced then, arms spread wide, he advanced on Curly, who had little room to move between the car and the wall. Curly threw a punch at Freddie which connected with his cheek. Shaking his head, Freddie kept advancing until he was close enough to grab him in a bear hug. Curly's feet left the ground as Freddie squeezed. A rib cracked. Then another. Curly gasped with pain and Freddie released him and, as Curly slumped against the car, he pushed past him and went into the hotel.

As he walked down to the little chemist on the main road, Curly felt almost grateful to Freddie for the agonising pain in his sides. It was a well-deserved retribution, and each careful breath he took sent a cathartic spasm through his torso and his conscience. Back in his room, he stripped to the waist and applied a wide strip of adhesive tape tightly around his ribcage. He had damaged various parts of his body over the years of practising dancing and had a crude but effective knowledge of patching up such injuries. There. That would do. A deep breath hurt as did a wide reaching out but it would mend.

Mary's support team, such as it was, continued to offer whatever support it could offer, even though acceptance of it was unsure at such a junction. Freddie was a member of that team. He drove out towards the Gap of Dunloe and, parking above the main viewing site, he walked up the slope until he came to a small spring around which, in the damp or boggy ground, various wildflowers had set down roots and flourished. When his mother was alive, she had sent him there regularly to collect them and make little bouquets for the dining room tables. He had always enjoyed these trips and grew to recognise and welcome the various flowers that came into bloom as the seasons progressed. There were, at various times of the year: anemones, white and pink, ragwort, buttercups and flowering heathers. He gathered a goodly and colourful selection and bound them and small green plants with long wisps of grass into a respectable and fragrant bunch and enjoyed the peacefulness of the pursuit and the soft wind that caressed his hair. Back in town that night, he went to Joy's cottage and knocked softly. She opened the door, glanced without comment at the bouquet and indicated Mary's room, before disappearing into the living room and closing the door. But not quite shut. Freddie approached Mary's door and knocked softly but there was no answer.

"Mary? Mary, it's Freddie. Wondering how you are."

There was no answer, so he sat down on the floor and leaned against the door.

"It's not easy talking to you through a closed door. Come to think of it, maybe it is. I… need you. I want you to become more involved in the hotel."

He nervously started to pick the blooms from the bouquet. Inside, Mary also sank to the floor against the door. Freddie cleared his throat and continued.

"I'm facing the biggest challenge in my life since my mother died; these dance auditions. I need help in the organisation of it all. And I think you're facing your biggest challenge – a dancer."

More blooms were picked and fell to the floor.

"I never said 'I told you so' but I told you so. Hinted anyway. Or tried to."

More blooms fell.

"I brought you some wild flowers, from the Gap of Dunloe."

Mary stifled a sob but he heard it.

"But the blooms seem to have come off."

He rose to his feet and looked at the stalks and greens.

"Maybe I'll give the stalks to Minnie."

He walked to the front door and let himself out, pulling the door shut behind him. Joy opened her door and watched him go. Mary's door opened and she came out. She saw the blooms on the floor and started to gather them up. Joy watched her silently.

***

The next morning, Artie was at his bench when Curly appeared, swaying slightly.

"Where have you been?"

"Busy."

"You've been drinking!"

119

"Good fucking guess. You must have had a secondary education."

"You're drunk!"

"Shit! There's no end to your brilliance. Were you at the… what do you call them… the Christian Brothers?"

"You're not fit to handle sharp tools!"

"No, I'm not. The Jesuits! I knew it. Only the Society of Jesus could produce such an intellectual pro-pro-gidy. No, that's wrong, prod-did-gy."

Curly picked up a drill, winced and rubbed his ribs, and then advanced on a stack of steel sheets.

"They've already been drilled" yelled Artie.

"And they're going to be drilled, pierced – *penetrated* – again."

Artie went off in search of the manager. Curly started his drilling.

"All right, you sixteenth-of-an-inch thick bastards" he hissed. "I'm going to drill your mild steel asses off."

He started to drill madly.

When Artie came back with the very nervous manager, Curly was rinsing his face at the sink, and propped up against the stack of sheets was the one he had worked on. 'GOODBYE' it read in rather crooked letters. Curly turned to face them.

"Artie," he said, "you're the best mild steel sheet – Christ, that's hard to say – measurer in this godforsaken country. I'm proud to have stood by your side and drilled your holes."

He made his dignified way out, winking at Smack on the way. Smack started to mutter:

"He's going. The big car. Gone. Can't go. Don't smack."

He rushed to the back of the shed where he had accumulated odd pieces of metal and an assortment of broken or damaged tools and started scrabbling around among them, muttering to himself:

"Fix it. Make a new one. Show him. Don't smack."

He started to beat a thin strip of mild steel in a circle.

120

"What the hell is he doing?" asked the manager.

"Leave him alone. He likes making things."

They both looked at the industrious Smack for a while as he struggled with the steel.

"What the hell! I think we're well rid of that Yank. He wasn't much use to us. Anyway, the job is finished."

The manager walked back towards his office. Artie continued to look at Smack who was trying to beat the ends of the steel strip together in a join. He walked over to him. Smack cringed.

"Don't smack," he muttered.

"I won't smack. I'll show you how to join the steel." He moved over to the soldering bench, beckoning Smack to follow him. He picked up the circle of mild steel.

"Is this... Oh, I see."

"Broken on the car. Don't smack. Fix it. Make a new one."

"Well, I'll help you. Lead. Get some lead while I get this going."

Smack scrabbled around on the shelves and located a small ingot of lead.

"That's it, Smack. That'll do it. Now, light that furnace."

They lit the furnace, and while it was heating up, Artie showed Smack how to cleave off a finger of lead of roughly the right dimensions. The he showed him how to hammer the lead gently into a bullet shape with points at both ends. Then they cut a sliver of steel, and when the furnace had heated up, Smack, under Artie's guidance, inserted it and took it out glowing red. With the hammer, he beat it into a thin, rounded column the right length to hold the lead bullet in the centre of the steel circle. With a flange at one end and a sharp point at the other, the column was soon joined to the bullet and the circle so that, when it was inserted into the bullet and soldered to the circle, it held the former in the exact centre. Artie took the finished fake mascot and told Smack to polish it until it shone.

"He'll like that," Artie said to a beaming Smack.

12

The payback

Mary lay on her bed, which was crumpled and untidy, unlike its usual almost pristine state. She was looking out through the window at a whitewashed wall on which the shadows of the leaves of a nearby oak tree danced and shifted in a hypnotic sequence. She had been watching this ever since the sun had risen over the surrounding roofs. There was a gentle knock on the door.

"Come in, Auntie Joy."

The door opened and Joy wheeled herself in. On her lap was a small tray containing a bowl of soup.

"I've made you some soup."

"You never cook."

"If I didn't, we'd both starve."

"Oh, Auntie Joy. I've been so selfish."

"You'll make amends by eating this."

She offered the soup and Mary, sitting on the edge of her bed, accepted it. She started eating, reluctantly at first, but with more satisfaction as the soup hit the spot. Joy watched with grim satisfaction for a while.

"I once stood as tall and straight next to a stove as I stood next to a man."

Mary started to speak but Joy silenced her with an impatient wave of her hand.

"Finish your soup. You have to get out of this room and out of Ballymalloy or you'll end up like me…" Mary looked at her in surprise "… an emotional and physical cripple. An appendage of a man, or what I remember of him."

Mary handed her the empty bowl.

"Now you can take me out to look at what remains of my man."

She wheeled herself out as Mary hurried to get up and dressed. Moments later, she was wheeling Joy out onto the street.

"Break off some of those roses for me, darling."

Mary did as she was told and they started out along the main street. For a while, they were silent. Joy was humming *Believe Me, If All Those Endearing Young Charms* under her breath.

"Thomas Moore?'

"Thomas Moore, the bard of Erin. I'm not tiring you, am I?"

"No. You're only a light old thing."

"Aye, that's true, but I used to be a right armful. Murphy said there was eating and drinking on me. He had his fill, that's for sure. Do you know he used to lay side bets on our dancing, without ever telling me? That we'd dance faster, longer, anything that could be measured. Made a small fortune, he did."

They reached the graveyard, turned in and made for Joe's grave, Joy was clutching the roses.

"You loved dancing," Mary said.

"And Murphy did too. He didn't deserve me as a partner of course. He was a scutter. A bollix."

Mary burst into shocked laughter as they reached Joe's grave. Joy started to throw the roses at the headstone.

"A double-dyed gurrier who should have been garrotted at puberty before his balls had time to fall out of him. Easy or you'll have me in the grave with him."

Mary calmed down slowly as Joy tossed the last rose in.

"The last rose of summer," she sighed.

"Another Moore song."

"Yes…"

"But you loved Joe all the same."

"Of course, I loved him. The bastard."

"What happened… after, Auntie Joy? You never told me."

"No. I never told anybody."

There was a long pause.

"I suppose I was waiting for the right time to tell you. And now that you are in a similar position, the time is as right as it will ever be." She sighed deeply. "One weekend, we won the dance contest at Cork so I… let him book us into the hotel there for the night. As Mr and Mrs Murphy. And I gave myself to him for the first time."

Mary held her breath.

"The next morning, he was gone. I didn't know where. And two months later, I discovered that I was pregnant."

Mary went pale.

"Life didn't seem worth it without him, and the thought of the baby, and the shame was… too much. So… I jumped off the viewing site at the Gap of Dunloe. It wasn't high enough, though. I suppose I knew that. I didn't die but I was hurt – badly. My back was a mess, they told me. It wasn't only the legs. They thought that my brain would stop working too. I was in a coma for a year. They lost all hope for me. Thought I would be a vegetable for the rest of my life. But I came out of it. The baby was gone of course. They had cut it out of me and put it up for adoption. Wouldn't tell me where, and to tell the God's honest truth, I didn't want to know, God forgive me. Never saw it again."

The silence was terrible and Mary clutched Joy's hand.

"Years later," Joy continued, "his family sent Joe back in a coffin. They didn't want to do the burying."

Mary winced as Joy's grip tightened.

"Make that American bastard get you up to his level, where you can win that bloody audition, and get to Dublin."

"But he.... he..."

"Make him pay, the bugger. Before it's too late. He's your only chance."

They stood there, silent, looking at the grave and the roses, both feeling angry at the prices women had had to pay over the centuries. Joy's anger was the lesser of the two. She had had many long, empty years to absorb and live with it. Mary's anger was still white hot, but it had altered since that terrible night when Curly had demonstrated his immaturity. Now there was room for vengeful thought and, aided by Joy's exhortation, she now knew what she must do, and as her resolve stiffened, so her anger abated. She deposited Joy at her house and prepared to leave for the hotel in a calmly determined way. She said nothing to Joy who guessed that something was afoot and that something boded ill – or did it? – for Curly. She went into the living room and looked at the photograph of Joe, but not in anger.

"Poor old Joe. You never made amends, probably never even confessed your sin. You might have died more easily if you had. It's strange, Joe, that we women have to do much for you men. And none of you deserve it."

***

When Mary reached the hotel, she made straight for Curly's room and stood outside for a moment, listening to the movements within.

Inside the room, Curly finished packing his suitcase, closed it and took up the box of records. The gramophone was already in the car. He surveyed the room, glad it was for the last time. He moved to the door, placed the suitcase on the ground and turned the handle. The door swung back to reveal Mary, arm raised to knock. She brushed past him, picked up the suitcase, threw it on the bed and opened it.

"Leaving town, are we?"

"Eh… yes."

She started to unpack the suitcase.

"You have some unfinished business with me to take care of before you leave."

Curly started to sputter in alarm.

"Look. You owe me." She started to place the clothing in the drawers, with more care than Curly had ever shown. "I don't know how many women you have seduced with your *Moonlight Serenade* routine. And I don't care. But I'm not going to pay the price alone. You're going to make amends."

"Listen. I'm not the marrying—"

"Oh, I don't want you to make me an honest woman."

She turned to him, with a jacket in her hands.

"I want you to make me a dancer. Where does this go?"

He pointed at the wardrobe.

"In there. I came here to get away from that world."

"The world you weren't good enough for?"

He stared to bridle, but she shoved a pair of shoes into his hands.

"Well, let me tell you—" he started to say.

"You weren't good enough to beat people like Darcy," she interrupted. "You're running away from him, but the world isn't big enough, and Ballymalloy is not far enough, not even in that shagging machine of yours."

"You're being ridiculous!" he said weakly, taking the trousers she thrust at him, hanging them in the wardrobe and placing the shoes at the bottom.

"No. You're the ridiculous one here, taking out your disappointment on me – and Minnie."

She slammed the wardrobe door, narrowly missing catching his fingers.

"You've given up, haven't you?"

She took the box of records off the bed and shoved them into his arms. He winced as the box hit his ribs.

"Well, you can't! Not until you make me good enough to win that contest."

She stormed out. The wardrobe door swung slowly open to reveal his reflection, standing in a shabby room at the ass end of the universe, being ordered around by a woman. He tried to close the door. Unsuccessfully.

"Jesus!" he said.

13

The shame

All over the world, in cities, towns and villages, a form of modern folklore developed and grew apace as people were thrust into closer and closer proximity with each other, from isolated cottages, to nascent villages, to developing towns and to increasingly complex cities. This folklore, mostly with a local focus, helped people come to terms with their fears, which were caused by rapidly changing lifestyles. One step above gossip and closely supported by it, these variations of the ancient ur-tales and myths were frequently of a threatening, sometimes of a reassuring or a cautionary nature. They featured the bad child, the wicked witch, the evil night stalker, etc. Such were the staple characters of the tales which were occasionally attached to real, living denizens of each habitat, often with devastating results. Ballymalloy was no different; it had its dimly understood but often retold stories over the years, one of which started when Smack came into the town, but the fact that the respected and admired parish priest, Father O'Grady, was the one who brought him in, curtailed the usual viciousness and hushed the hiss of scandal, even though Smack carried the name of O'Grady. Smack, being a pitiable creature, soon became a focus of the town's philanthropic aspirations, especially because acts of charity towards him were very economical.

***

Joy was in the graveyard again, directing Smack in his efforts to clean up Joe's grave and trim the long grass around it with clippers. He had just finished it to her satisfaction when Father O'Grady approached. Joy gave Smack a sixpenny piece and patted his hand.

"You're a good man, Smack, and you help me a lot. Thank you."

Smack turned away, bowing to the priest as he hurried to the shop to spend his tanner. He was muttering to himself as usual.

"Good woman. Gave me a tanner. Liquorish or gum drops? Both. Last all day. Good Father. Talking to her. Wonder what. Maybe toffee. Last longer. Bad for teeth, Father says. Don't care. Lasts all day."

Off he went, lost in dreams of sweets. Father O'Grady sat on a gravestone facing Joy.

"I'm told you wanted to see me. Here I am."

"I want you to hear my confession."

"You haven't been to confession since…"

"Since the accident."

"Since the accident," he agreed.

"I can't bear the thought of that confessional of yours. It's like a tomb."

"Well, this is just as good. Peaceful. It draws your thoughts to death. And judgement."

"It's no use looking crossways at me like that."

"Well, what's bothering you, my child?"

"I slept with Joe, I tried to kill myself and I gave up my child. How's that for a start?"

129

"Well, you've done your penance for it all, and it just remains for me to absolve you."

"Just like that?"

"Just like that. Confession consists of repentance, contrition and a firm desire of amendment. All of which I assume you feel."

"Oh yes. Certainly all."

"Well then, I can absolve you of your sins and send you away in peace."

"It all seems so… offhand."

"Listen, my child." The priest allowed himself a feeling of irritation. "I knew all this. I was there, remember. And I know how much pain you went through. And desolation. Neither of which justifies the sins but it does explain them. It was thirty years ago and you've been in your own private hell since, and now that you have finally asked God for forgiveness, I give you absolution freely and with a glad heart. Now do you remember the Act of Contrition?"

"Oh yes."

"Well, say it."

And she said the prayer, with a fuller heart than she had expected. The priest, meanwhile, was hurled back to the time when he almost gave up his vocation.

He had been there when she was brought back from the Gap of Dunloe, her body broken and bleeding. All hope of her surviving was gone and he had administered Extreme Unction to a woman he thought was on the edge of eternity, but her years of dancing had toughened her body, and slowly she recovered, as did the unborn child in her womb. She herself remained in a coma for the best part of a year. He had organised her movement to a convent in Tuam run by the Bon Secours Sisters, where she was delivered of a baby boy by caesarean section. The boy was bent and deformed and was placed in the Mother and Baby Home run by the same order of nuns. The priest had kept an eye on him, sporadically visiting the home over the next few years until the memory faded and he concluded that the boy was receiving the best treatment he could have hoped for from a caring Church. Joy came home, crippled but resolved to rebuild her life. She never expressed any desire to know about her child, and slowly the memory receded in her life and that of the priest.

Until one day a young man came to see the priest in Ballymalloy, bearing news that Father O'Grady instantly perceived as a burden he would have to bear for the rest of his life.

"Father O'Grady. My name is Finbarr O'Neill. I am – was – a priest. I need to speak to you. In total confidence."

"Whether I can guarantee total confidence or not depends on what you have to tell me. But come in, please. Have a cup of tea."

"I'd… I'd rather have a drink. If you don't mind."

"Fine, come in."

Over a glass of whiskey, the young man poured out his story in a torrent of angry words interspersed by tearful pauses. The priest listened with increasing concern which turned to sadness as the loss to the Catholic Church of this intelligent and moral man became clearer.

"I had always wanted to be a priest, ever since I first received Holy Communion. I thought what a marvellous thing it was that I could do to forgive individual people their sins and then to give the body and blood of Christ to a whole congregation, knowing that I was offering them salvation. Besides…" he took another drink "… my parents were persuaded by the parish priest that one of their children offered to the Church would ensure their entry into heaven."

There was a long pause before Finbarr could continue, and Father O'Grady was reminded of the same excitement and acceptance with which his parents had listened to the blandishments of their parish priest so long ago.

"I had a challenging but fulfilling time at the seminary in Maynooth. When I was first ordained, I was sent to Tuam Cathedral in Galway and I was very excited. It is a lovely church with a magnificent vault, and on the rare occasions I was allowed to say mass at the main altar, I was proud, very proud, to be a priest and part of a great and holy tradition. The Archbishop was a small but very convivial man, always ready for a drink and a chat after supper and things were very satisfying for about a year…"

***

The Archbishop sat at the end of his highly-polished table with Father O'Neill at the far end and a pimply young novice on the Archbishop's left. A bowl of simmering oxtail soup had been placed in front of each of them by a tall, thin and obsequious butler who now stood absolutely motionless behind the Archbishop's high-backed chair.

"Father O'Neill, for the first of your onerous duties in my parish, would you please say grace."

"Yes, your Grace. Certainly." He bowed his head and started to say the rather lengthy grace he was used to hearing at Maynooth but, halfway through, the Archbishop coughed and raised his wine glass.

"Thank you, Finbarr, the intention is often sufficient. Taste this *Pouilly-Fuissé*. It goes rather well with the oxtail, don't you think?"

The two priests sipped and were duly appreciative. Finbarr had never tasted such a sublime wine and his Grace was right. It did compliment the oxtail, superbly.

"Makes a change from mulligatawny, don't you think?" said the Archbishop, who had disposed of his soup and his first glass of wine by the time Finbarr had tasted his third spoonful. "Finbarr – no, no, continue with your soup, mustn't waste it – you'll find it's all very relaxed here in Tuam. I flatter myself that the Archdiocese gets all due respect and reverence, so I never have to exert myself in that regard. The various churches and religious houses around here report to me regularly and I never have cause to complain.

Ah, here's the sirloin. Help yourselves. We have some fine old claret to wash it down."

Having being served first, the Archbishop loaded his plate with the meat and poured over it some dark, rich gravy. Then he gulped the first glass of the wine that had been poured and added potatoes and greens to the generous helping from the plates that had been arrayed around him in a reverent semicircle. He started to eat before the others had finished serving themselves and carried on speaking, often with his mouth full.

"I have a particularly soft spot for the Mother and Baby Home which is efficiently run by the Bon Secours Sisters under the… rather forceful, shall I say… Mother Bridget who, although very strict, has a heart of gold and never fails to admit to me that she loves her charges, mothers and children, to a fault. To a fault. How is the steak? Fine? Good. And the claret? Excellent."

The Archbishop helped himself to more steak from the promptly proffered platter and allowed his glass to be recharged.

"The other establishment I am rather proud of is the Industrial School run by the Christian Brothers. There are over a hundred boys in its charge and I particularly require you, Finbarr, to look after their spiritual needs. Their physical needs are adequately addressed by the Holy Church, but their souls need some careful and loving attention. We would be remiss in our Christ-given duties if we neglected such matters. So, Finbarr, I would like you to devote some considerable time and energy to those two charitable places of refuge."

Finbarr, of course, wholeheartedly agreed and was asked to share a glass of wine with the Archbishop in agreement.

***

Finbarr took another drink from Father O'Grady and continued, but there was a tremble in the hitherto firm and confident voice.

"… I threw myself into these duties willingly and soon realised

133

that I would have to use the name and support of the Archbishop when my attempted ministrations to the inmates were subtly foiled, or when meetings with them were either cancelled or overseen by a nun or a brother, in spite of my objections. I was always informed that such were the orders from above, and when I tried to address them through meetings with those responsible, such meetings were either cancelled at the last minute, or those whom I did meet pleaded ignorance of the matter or the inmates I wanted to meet. It was frustrating but, in my ignorance, I attributed it to incompetence or lack of insight. However, I was active in my duties as I perceived them and began to be relentless in my requests and more forceful in my demands. This was because I grew increasingly uneasy about the rumours, however faint, that were circulating about the home and the school. They were like early autumn breezes that shiver the trees and scatter the leaves over the land, but they were hard to pin down. Hard to see coming and hard to feel passing. But when they passed, the land was always emptier. Always emptier. More desolate."

The young man spoke as if he had recounted these feelings before but found them more painful at each telling. He paused again, this time for a longer period, and the priest didn't want him to continue but he knew he would, and he knew that he was deeply obligated to listen. Out it came; visits to the home strenuously resisted by the Mother Superior of the nuns and the Brother Superior of the industrial school. Excuses and cancelled appointments grew increasingly frequent, and Finbarr became so suspicious that he set up surreptitious contacts with the young boys from the school and furtive meetings with the older ones out of whom he managed to get some of the truth.

"When I tried to make my first contacts, I was dismayed at the suspicion I was faced with. I'm the eldest in a large family and I was always capable of creating relationships with children; healthy and carefree children that is. But a dim picture began to emerge, once I had managed to build up some trust among the boys, of what was going on in the school. I started with the industrial school and when I began to make discrete enquiries, I was resisted, even castigated, by the Brothers. These, remember, were celibate men, denied of the priesthood and a normal life from their early teens as indeed was I. But I had the consolation of priestly powers."

The story came out in a torrent: Finbarr's confrontation with widespread secrecy, coupled with active, poisonous antagonism from the nuns and Brothers as well as angry denials by all who did business with them. But he persisted and gradually became aware that, far from providing a supportive environment, as demanded by their mandate from society and from Jesus, both establishments were operating brutal systems of penal servitude; laundries, workshops and the sale of free and lucrative labour to nearby farms, all supplemented by generous grants from the Church.

"The farm labour was the worst. The boys were dropped at the farms and left to the mercy of the individual farmers. At night, at the end of their daily labours, they were locked in the barns, sometimes even among the pigs, and the most awful food was left out for them. I heard of a particular farm that had been using the boys for several years and decided to find out for myself. One night, I went to this farm and crept up to the old barn where I had been told the boys were held overnight. I whispered to them through the sagging planks and, after a while, one of the older boys took courage, answered me and poured it all out. They had been working there for three days, harvesting the turnips in the fields furthest away from the roads. Their only sustenance was the crop itself, gnawed when the overseers weren't looking, and washed down by water from the cow trough in the adjacent field. Three ragged farm labourers served as overseers each had a massive and wild dog on a leash which they would let slip at the first sign of insubordination. At night, when locked in the barn, cast iron buckets full of rough swills of chopped turnips and other boiled vegetables, mostly stalks, were put inside the doors for them to eat from. By morning, their thirsts were so raging they would stampede to the horse trough in the barnyard and bury their faces in the awful water. One night, a boy called Tom had escaped and the rest were beaten to try to elicit information about him. But they knew nothing and Tom was never heard from again."

During that time, hints emerged, however dim and clouded by fear, of unmerciful beatings, of the indiscriminate and arbitrary chastisement with the 'blackjack', an 18-inch strip of many layered leather, studded with coins and other pieces of metal by the Brothers, and the heavy wooden rosaries by the nuns, unexplained departures of boys and girls, abuse of a terrible, unmentionable nature, especially of the boys. He started to create a dossier of the abuse and wicked practices inflicted on the children and young girls and boys, and it was explosive. It contained details of what he had heard and what he had seen, and he fervently believed it would be taken seriously by the Church and would prompt at least an enquiry by someone more experienced than he. Then came the breaking point for him: a cynical – and sinful – mockery of the sacrament of confession. It was the final straw for Finbarr. Using his close connection with the bishop as his credentials and leverage, he had managed to organise the hearing of confession among the older girls at the home who were mostly in their stunted early teens.

"It was about this time that I realised I was dealing with such a degree of obfuscation, deceit and immoral twisting of the rules as to amount to disobedience to the wishes, as I thought, of the Archbishop. I had insisted on hearing the confessions of the girls in the Mother and Child Home and would not take 'no' for an answer. The Mother Superior finally gave in, or seemed to."

To his horror, he witnessed the terror of the girls when they were brought into the allotted room attended by a bevy of nuns and when he insisted on shriving them, the most the grim faced and grudging Mother Superior would allow was a 'group confession'. The girls were instructed to review their sins silently and, after a group Act of Contrition, led by the Mother Superior, he was allowed grant group absolution. He went back to the Archbishop's mansion in a rage and demanded an audience. The Archbishop was busy? Then he would wait. No, he would not come back at a more convenient hour, he would wait. In the meantime, would the minion kindly hand this dossier to the Archbishop? It was taken from him as if it contaminated and bourn reluctantly away. And wait he did, in the gloomy cavernous, gloomy reception room for three hours before he was shown into the Archbishop's study. Unknown to him, the Mother Superior from the home and the Brother Superior of the industrial school had asked for and were granted an urgent audience. So, when Finbarr entered the study, gone was the boozy bonhomie, gone was the twinkling eye and the soft phrase. This was a very senior member of the Church hierarchy, whose authority had been challenged by a newly minted priest from Maynooth, barely out of his novitiate! His anger was not concealed. Never before had he been flouted, lied to, manipulated. And by a whippersnapper.

"How dare you!" he shouted at the priest when he entered. It was then Finbarr knew that his efforts at righting a terrible wrong were over; indeed, so perhaps was his priesthood. The raging prelate was waving Finbarr's dossier around and brandishing it as if it were a faggot to light the fire under a heretic.

"What is this filth? This calumny? This sin against Christ! Against the Holy Ghost! Against the sanctity and benevolence of the Holy Roman and Apostolic Church!"

He threw the dossier into the fire that was burning in the capacious grate and watched it burst into flames with grim satisfaction.

"Thus!' he roared. "Thus, do I consign to flames your lies and false accusations. Thus, do I refute and anathematise you."

"It would have been funny," said Finbarr to Father O'Grady,

"this fat, sleek sybaritic dwarf screaming as if he were a Savonarola cleansing the earth for a new Jerusalem. But I was full of overwhelming sadness; for the children, for their errant guardians and for the Church – and for me with my dreams of holy priesthood demolished."

The Church, when it discovered his actions, thoughts and disillusionment, carried out a vindictive series of censures. First of all, he was suspended, which prohibited his carrying out many clerical acts and powers conferred on him by his ordination. This would remain in force until he showed repentance! When he refused to repent for the acts of his colleagues, there was an act of laicisation which dismissed him from the clerical state entirely.

"I am so angry, Father O'Grady. Not only because of what they denied me but, more importantly, about the treatment of the boys and girls who were given to us to care for in the spirit of Jesus Christ who said, 'Suffer little children to come unto me, and forbid them not: for of such is the kingdom of God.' But these… godless… people make the children suffer! And when they heard about it from me, made *me* suffer. Is this Christianity, Father? Is this the religion I longed to be a part of and studied so much to make myself worthy of it? I feel so… helpless… and dirty because I did nothing about it. Nothing worthwhile."

"Why did you come here to me to tell me this?"

"Because you're a priest!" Finbarr's anger was palpable.

"Yes. I am a priest and I am ashamed of what is happening in my name and in the name of Jesus Christ."

"Then do something."

"Yes! But what?"

He saw the sceptical look on Finbarr's face. "I don't know right now. But I will do what is within my power. I promise you… and the great God above… that I will do what I can."

"Your name is on record at the Mother and Baby Home" Finbarr continued when he had more command of himself. "I don't know what for. The details are deliberately vague. But it appears to me that you did participate at some stage, perhaps with good, but ignorant, intentions but now that.... you *do* believe me?"

"It's impossible not to believe you."

And indeed, it was. The sincerity and deep-rooted anguish of the young man was beyond doubt. Father O'Grady crossed himself and muttered a short but fervent phrase of prayer.

"I know you will do what you can. Now I must go," said Finbarr.

"Where?"

"Wherever the Christ of the little children takes me. I seek priests like you, Father, to awaken and, hopefully, to act. Thanks for the drink."

He paused at the door and turned back to the priest.

"Does God curse people?"

He left and the priest was in turmoil. There was little enough he could do to stop the abuse, much as that dismayed him, but the one thing he could do – *had* to do – was to rescue the young boy he had handed over to the care of the nuns. The boy was now, if he was still living, in his early teens, and when the priest arrived at the Cathedral of the Assumption of the Blessed Virgin Mary in Tuam the next day, with Finbarr's pain infecting his very bones, he was admitted into the presence of the Archbishop to whom he communicated his mission; to find the boy he had committed to the care of the Mother and Baby Home so many years ago. He had given the boy his own name, Declan O'Grady, and when he told this to the Archbishop, he was horrified when the cleric winked conspiratorially and handed him on to his assistant with many nods of the head and what, in a less elevated mortal, would have been sniggers. O'Grady left the cathedral feeling sick, horrified and contaminated. The assistant dived into the sparse files that existed and managed to trace the boy to the nearby industrial school to which he had been transferred at the tender age of five. *Five!* thought O'Grady. *How could I have been so casual, so uncaring and so blind? Dear Christ, forgive me and help me undo some of the damage I have done.*

At the dismal and forbidding reformatory, after many and persistent enquiries, he was finally allowed to see the boy, and the meeting almost unmanned him. The boy had acquired the name Smack because every time he sensed some antagonism, and there were plenty of times, he would cringe behind his raised arms and mutter "Don't smack." He was painfully thin and obviously malnourished, and his skinny arms and bare legs bore the wounds of many beatings. He was dressed in rags and he stank. He had had no education of any sort and was treated like an animal by everyone, including his fellow inmates who were pleased, in a feral way, to have somebody worse off than they. So had the grim regime bled all sense of humanity out of the boys. Feeling unclean himself, Father O'Grady took the boy back to Ballymalloy and presented him to his housekeeper who, with brusque and down-to-earth kindness, bathed him thoroughly, cut his hair and nails and dressed him in clothes hurriedly purchased from the local outfitters. Then she and the priest embarked on the slow process of teaching him how to behave in normal surroundings among normal people.

When he had gotten used to life in the priest's house and the church environments, they slowly introduced him into town life. Smack grew into a less tormented but still damaged man, and between the factory, where the priest had organised a job for him, and the priest's house, he carried out many easy duties, treated with respect by all and eventually the casual affection that small, insulated communities generally bestow on those less fortunate. Smack's pride and joy was the massive metal delivery bike that the priest bestowed on him, and he soon became a fixture in Ballymalloy as he whizzed around the streets at high speeds. Joy also employed him occasionally, totally unaware of their true relationship.

In this manner, Smack built up a support group of kindly

people, became as happy as such a damaged person could be, and Father O'Grady atoned somewhat for his ungodly neglect. He lavished loving care on Smack which assuaged his conscience somewhat, but each night, as he knelt down to pray, a whiff of shame came to him which brought forcibly to mind the efforts, hopeless as they would probably prove to be, of Finbarr O'Neill's crusade to rouse the priests of Ireland. Father O'Grady knew only too well how impossible that would be. The Church's grip was too tight, the stakes were too high and the mighty men at the pinnacle of Catholic power were too proud to admit to allowing such ecclesiastical abuse in the name of Christ.

14

The lessons

The dining room had been reorganised to create a decent-sized space for dancing in one corner. Curly's gramophone and the stack of records were on a table to one side, and Mary was scattering French chalk on the floor. Freddie was helping her spread it by dragging his feet through it as he walked up and down. He tested the slipperiness of it and almost lost his balance.

"Oops! It's slippery," he said.

"That's the general idea."

She too shuffled up and down in the centre of the cleared space.

"Have to get rid of it when dinner is served. Can't have the Smiths zooming up and down."

"It'll sweep off easily enough."

"Do you think you can do it?" asked Freddie, after a pause.

"If those flat-footed policemen can play jazz, I can dance to it."

"I suppose it has to be with him?"

"Who else? Can you teach me?"

"It's just that…"

"Don't worry; it's payback time. He'll behave, I can promise you. Hello, Mr Collins."

"Mary. Freddie."

Freddie nodded and got out of the room.

"Mary, why the formality?"

"This is a business relationship, Mr Collins. Shall we start?'

He walked up to her and held out his left hand, fingers loosely cupped. She placed her right hand in his.

"Relax your fingers. Just let those three fingers rest there."

He moved his hand to swing her from side to side. She was stiff at first but relaxed into it.

"This is the centre of it all. The centre of your universe."

She smiled at this but he remained deadly serious.

"With these three fingers, I can control the weight, the speed and the momentum of a woman's body. Doesn't matter how fat or clumsy or heavy she is."

The swaying got bigger and built up a rhythm. He moved his weight from foot to foot and she followed. He switched hands, her left in his right and back again. The same cupped fingers, now only two.

"Have you ever fenced?"

She shook her head.

"You hold a fencing foil balanced on two fingers, like that. Totally relaxed. Ready for the thrust with your full weight behind it. Like that."

He pressed his thumb firmly on her fingers, turned his hand so that the palm faced downwards and thrust her away into a spin. She twirled and her hand came back into his. But clumsily and she lost the rhythm.

"Jesus, Mary!" he said.

"And Joseph," she countered. "Sorry."

"Okay. The rules are: one beat at a time, one step at a time and one move at a time. Each must be clear in both our minds, but they must look seamless and spontaneous to whoever is watching.

He turned her slowly but rhythmically, their hands touching, holding lightly, slipping in and out of each other's; above her head, behind her back, even behind his back, the cupped hand was always there. Their arms performed arabesques, slowly, slowly, slowly as he spoke.

"This is as much about getting used to each other as it is about jiving. Close your eyes."

She did and gave herself over to the dancing.

"When you're fly fishing, the rod is like another arm. There's no strength in your grip as you get ready to cast. Maybe just your little finger. The rod just lies there, perfectly balanced. The line slipping through the fingers."

He took her upper arm and as she slowly turned, let it slide out through his loose hand until her fingers came back into his."

"Until the fish bites."

His fingers stopped the spin and pushed her whole body into reverse. She spun several times as she moved slowly away. He followed and at the right moment, his fingers were there in exactly the right place to stop her spinning. They stood there, motionless, fingers loosely clasped.

"Well?" she asked.

"You might have the potential. Now you have to learn to trust."

"Trust."

"Yes. You have to trust that the man will be there. Every time. Got it?"

"Got it."

He spun her several times.

"Now we've got to read each other's minds. You've got to know how far I want you to spin, so that I'm there at the end. You've got to trust the beat and trust that I'll be there."

He spun her away forcefully and walked to the far side of the dancing space. Her hand came into his and he spun her back again. Again the walk, again the catch.

Outside in reception, Freddie stepped forward as Mr and Mrs Smith headed for the dining room.

"Aah. Good morning, Mr and Mrs Smith. I'm afraid you can't go in there just yet."

"Why ever not?" Mrs Smith wanted to know.

"Because, some… stuff… has been put on the floor and it will be sometime before the… fumes go away."

He started to usher them towards the bar.

"Anyway, I'd like your opinion on what I've done in the bar."

"But we never go into the bar!"

Mr Smith looked as if he had led a life of deprivation.

"I know you don't," said Freddie. "But you have such good taste and I value your opinion."

He ushered them in and seated them at one of three tables he had arranged in the redecorated bar. Mrs Smith looked around critically.

"I'd have chosen a quieter colour for the walls, and some flowers would lighten the place up. But…"

Freddie really looked as if he was hanging on her every word.

"But?"

"We like it. Don't we, Smith?"

"Aah, erm, yes. I suppose—"

"That's settled then. The usual, please, Freddie."

"Right away."

***

Later that day, and every afternoon for the rest of the week, Mary and Curly practised in Joy's living room. The furniture had been pushed back against the wall and the rugs rolled up and stored in Mary's bedroom. He was relentless and demanding, pushing her harder and harder. When he wasn't spinning her, he was forcing her to hold ballet poses until her calves ached, her ankles throbbed and she protested agonisingly as she contorted in impossible bends and contortions. But she soon got through what Curly called the 'boot camp' stage, and her resilient and healthy body started to respond to the gruelling regimen with a greater flexibility and strength.

"Feel the signal, woman! No! You anticipated. You can do it, you know you can. That's it. Better. Better. But not good enough yet. Again. Again. Again."

"When do we do this to music?"

"When you're ready. Now spin."

Curly was benefitting from the practising too. He hadn't felt this good in years. If it weren't for his ribs, he would have been proud of his strength, his grace and his masculinity. They went into footwork and he made her practise basic tap steps, slowly at first and then faster and faster. Her training in Irish dancing was a huge advantage; she could move her feet fast. Very fast. And keep up an impressive heel and toe taps. When he got to teaching her tap, an integral part of jive and bop, he soon found out that she could adapt her *rince* routines to the new style. The main problem was that she automatically and instinctively adopted the formal Irish dancing style; body upright, arms straight down, preferably slightly behind her back, staring out in front. Curly was having none of this and dismissed *rince* as a possible source of style. In fact, he ordered her to try to drive *rince* out of her mind and concentrate on the loose, supple jazz dance style. She obeyed him but secretly she thought that there were so many parallels between the two styles that an amalgamation would be beneficial in some way.

All through these sessions, Joy sat outside the door listening and dying to look in but, when she asked, Curly rejected the idea, thinking that she would be a distraction. But secretly Joy knew better and thought long and hard about how she could change his mind.

***

One afternoon, Curly decided to up the style.

"Now I'm going to try something new. It's a sort of standard move-in jive, but I'm not sure you're ready for it yet. Watch this."

He stood facing her, with his legs apart and his hands on her hips. Then he took a pace backwards to demonstrate.

"I'm going to swing you between my legs. You are going to thrust your legs forward as if you were on a swing."

He crouched and demonstrated.

"I'm going to grab you and swing you back as far as I can. My elbows will be on my thighs for leverage and because I'm not strong enough to support your body weight. When I swing you back, I'll use the momentum of your body to get you right up there, as far as I can reach. It's the basic jive throw."

He gazed at her, somewhat anxiously, but she was all eagerness. He held her by the waist and she launched herself between his spread thighs. He swung her back, forward and upwards, but halfway through the lift, he gasped and brought her back down, holding his sides.

"What's the matter?" Mary asked.

"Nothing."

"Let me see."

"It's nothing. We're not ready. Okay. It's time… for this."

He moved to the records and the gramophone.

"At last!"

He put on *Peanut Vendor* and took her hand as the pounding music filled the room.

"*Peanut Vendor*. Stan Kenton, recorded in 1947. It's Cuban music. We're going to focus on it. Tell the story of it in dance. Not just random jive moves but a progression of dance sequences."

They started to move to the rhythmic guitar intro.

"That trombone. Hear how it takes over? We'll start to spin – there. Not too flashy. Controlled and holding back. That's it. Now when it moans, we dip. Three times, with the music. Like that. And that. And that."

They started to move more decisively.

"Now when the rest of the brass comes in, we pick up more speed. Lots of reverses in the spins. There's a battle going on in the brass section between the trumpets and the trombones and

147

we must echo that. Now, where it gets more expansive, we get flashier. Swinging wider and wilder. Maybe you leave me and go around the floor with me following. Now that dissonance. That's great. We need to work out some really great and unexpected moves for that section. We'll work on it. Now – a big ending and a dramatic stop. With the throw on the final beat. We won't do it now but later!"

They stopped and Mary felt a tingling all over her body. For the first time, jazz made complete and absolute sense to her. It was as if she had never danced before. She stood there breathing fast but controllably. She saw Joy looking in through the open door and there were tears in her eyes as she clasped her hand up against her throat.

"Now I want you to play that number again and again until you know every note, every beat. It's got to be in your blood because you and I are going to do it full justice. What the hell are you wearing?"

Mary had twirled so violently that her striped knickers came into view.

"What…?"

"Give me those panties. NOW!"

Shocked into acquiescence, she took off her knickers and handed them to him. He crunched them up in his hand.

"No stripes. No spots. No patterns. Plain. Always plain and always matching the dress. Okay?"

He thrust the knickers into her hand and left the room. Mary and Joy looked at each other. Mary in a state of shock. Joy trying to hide a grin.

"Cup of tea?" she asked.

***

That evening, Curly, Mary and Joy, who refused to be left out, were at the police cell, listening to the band as it ended *In the Mood*. Curly sighed deeply. The band looked at him blearily.

"It's not bad. I mean, if you improve at this rate, it'll do. Sort of. But…"

"But what?" Moriarty asked, somewhat put out.

"The sound is not big enough. The sound has to drive the dance, move the audience, get the crowd in the mood. What it really needs is…"

"What?"

"A wind section, at least another clarinet and about three or four saxophones. And a couple more trombones wouldn't do any harm."

"There's nobody else around here who plays any sort of music, never mind jazz."

"There's St Patrick's in Cork."

"The reformatory?'"

"Them bowsies would have the eyes out of your head."

"The thing is," said Moriarty, "I was talking to Brother Nestor a while back. He says his band there can play anything. They're so scared of him, they can even play calypso."

"What's that?"

Curly butted in.

"It's a Caribbean music. Good stuff. Just what we all need."

"Yeah. Like this," said the drummer as he played a calypso rhythm.

"Now you're talking," said Curly. "See if they're available."

He started to leave with Mary.

The saxophone spoke up.

"But they're delinquents!"

"And we're drunk." said Moriarty. "I'll see Nestor tomorrow morning."

Curly turned at the door.

"By the way, I want you all to work seriously on *Peanut Vendor*. Okay?"

15

The reformatory

When Mary walked into Minnie's front room, Minnie went into a mild state of panic.

"Mary... Mary... Mary."

"Yes. It's me. Hello."

"Hello... glad to see you... erm... cup of tea?"

"That'd be nice."

Minnie went into the tea-making part of her workshop and started to make tea, clumsily. Mary watched her for a while and then took over.

"Let me. Please."

With relief, Minnie relinquished the tea-making implements and moved to the window. She looked out and suddenly turned to Mary.

"Remember the first time we saw him in that car?"

"I do. It was as if the circus had come to town."

"It had. With Curley as the chief juggler. What a car though."

"There we were, two convent girls seduced by a fecking Buick."

"The nuns were right." Minnie continued, looking at Mary

closely. "The world is full of men wanting to commit immodest actions with pure young Irish girls."

"Yes. We were that. Once."

"Sister Gonzaga was right. She always said I would come to no good." Minnie giggled.

"Sister Gonzaga. What a name!"

"A Jesuit saint, of course."

"Of course. The nuns always had soft spot for the Js."

"But Gongaza! It sounds like some sort of disease you'd catch…"

"In the back seat of a Buick." Mary sighed. "One hour to Dublin."

"And one minute to the back seat."

They both buried their initial embarrassment in laughter. While they did, the tea was made and poured. They sipped a while before Minnie spoke.

"You're dancing with him for the auditions."

"Yes."

"How is it?"

"Great. Strictly business."

"Do you have a chance?"

"Yes. But that's all it is. I need a new dress."

Minnie got all business-like.

"And I get to make it?"

"Of course. Who else in this town?"

"Great. I finally get to make the dress I've always wanted to see you in."

Minnie dived into her pile of samples and pulled out a vivid green sample.

"How about this colour. It'll bring out the colour of your hair.

"No. It reminds me of the apples we used to steal from the nun's orchard."

"Oh, God, yeah. They were never ripe. I always got the runs after we'd eaten them."

"They were Grannie Smiths. They're not supposed to be ripe."

"And the gooseberries! They were always bitter too. I suppose it's because the nuns used to grow them. Bitter nuns – bitter fruit."

They were both silent, thinking of the convent.

"You got out of school early."

"That's because Auntie Joy took me in. You had to stay until the leaving."

"Yes. It was awful lonely without you." Minnie stared out through the window. "They wanted me to stay in the system, manage the laundry. Imagine that." She shuddered. "Those poor girls were like ghosts, thin and white."

"Yes. They looked horrible. Hopeless kind of. I got whipped for giving one of them a sweet."

"Gonzaga?"

"Gonzaga." Mary shook herself.

"It's got to be flame red." Said Minnie.

"My God!"

"Just to spite Gonzaga. And… "

"Sexy?"

"Yes. Well… "

"Flame red. I can't believe it. Oho! Look at this."

She produced a vibrant, flame red sample and held it up against Mary.

"A full skirt, so it swirls straight out."

"Well ..."

"Listen girl, you may as well be hung for a sheep as a lamb. They're going to gawk at you anyway, so give them an eyeful."

Mary giggled and grinned at the same time.

"And a neckline down to *here*," said Minnie "When the honour of Ballymalloy is at stake, what the feck's a little modesty? Erm… I'm seeing him. Do you mind?"

"No. I'm glad."

"It's just that… I thought you might still—"

"I'm glad. It's easier to concentrate on the dancing when the man isn't being led by his middle leg. By the way, I'll need flame red knickers as well."

Minnie was startled for a moment. Then she shrieked with delighted laughter.

"I'd love to see Sister Gonzaga's face. Should we exhume her?"

***

Artie was drilling the first of a new supply of mild steel sheets when Curly came into the shed.

"Artie, how's the new mild steel?"

"What do you want?"

"A favour."

"Why should I do you a favour?"

"Because I drilled a million holes for you. I stood side by side with you and helped fulfil your quota and keep your unblemished ten-year-old record. Come on, Artie, I'm just not cut out for that intense, demanding work."

"What's the favour?"

"The Buick. It got… dented. You're the only man I'd trust it to."

"The Buick?" Artie was impressed.

"The thing is, I need it for after the dance auditions."

"Oh yeah. I heard you were going in for that. Where's the car?"

"In the street."

They both headed for the gate. Smack stuck his head around the shed door and watched them go. The Buick looked a trifle off-kilter, with the crumpled mascot and the deep dent in the bodywork. Artie walked around it, looking at the damage.

"Well, the mascot is what we call in the trade, fucked. There's no repairing that. I don't suppose you could get another one?"

"In Ireland? I'd have to get one shipped out from the States, and that would take a long time."

Artie stroked the dent.

"Good thing it's black. I could beat that out; the metal is sound. And with some careful spraying and polishing, I could get it looking almost as new. I could fill up the hole where the mascot was and… Hold on. Smack!" he called without looking around.

Smack's head appeared around the gate post.

"Bring out that thing you made for the Buick." Smack's head disappeared. "You'll get a laugh out of this," Artie said to Curly.

Smack reappeared with his hands behind his back. Artie held out his hand and slowly Smack delivered the roughly made mascot. Artie offered it to Curly who looked at it in amazement for seconds while Smack stared at him. Then he roared with laughter.

"Smack! You're a genius. It's terrific! It'll look great there." He held the particularly ugly artefact on the hood. "Look! Buick themselves wouldn't know the difference. Artie, do the panel beating and then install this magnificent mascot, and Smack and I will ride through the town and show it off. Smack, hold on to it for now. We'll put it on when Artie has worked his magic."

Smack took the mascot and headed back into the factory, grinning widely.

"I've never seen him look so happy," said Artie. "It's going to look very, very quare."

"Quare is the name of the game from now on, Artie. And there's another little thing."

He produced a pair of black high heel shoes and a flame red cloth sample from the glove compartment.

"Can you mix that exact shade of red?"

"Artie sighed and took the shoes and sample.

"Anything else you want?"

"No. That's enough for now. Thanks."

He got into the Buick and drove away. Artie looked after him and shook his head ruefully.

*****

Thanks to the good offices of Father O'Grady, it was arranged that Moriarty and Curly could co-opt six boys from the band at the St Patrick's Reformatory in Upton in County Cork. It had recently been changed to an Industrial School, but the brutal regime hadn't altered. Transport to and from Ballymalloy was also arranged so Moriarty and his men, with Curly in tow, went to the reformatory to inspect the band there.

It was a grim stone building, surrounded by pine trees and a large expanse of particularly gritty and noisy gravel. As they walked across the gravel, Curly's teeth were set on edge by the noise. The hall into which they were escorted was cold and damp, with faded photographs and etchings of past Brother Superiors on the slimy walls, and on the stage, three rows of music stands and accompanying chairs faced them. Each of Moriarty's musicians had his bottle or flask secreted about their persons or in their capacious music bags. The damp atmosphere called for some sustenance, so the various vessels were brought into play as they gathered their instruments and sheet music and positioned themselves on the stage. The drummer set up his kit at the rear on a low dais and they all waited for the boys. Soon enough, the sound of marching and counting approached along the corridor, and into the hall came a smartly stepping line of boys, each with a musical instrument and a music folder. Closing up the rear was a small but well-set Brother with a pair of piercing blue eyes. He was doing the counting in a very loud voice.

"*Do, cathar. Do, Cathar. Do, Cathar. Staaa… dig!*"

The boys came to an abrupt halt, each staring straight ahead.

"All right. All right," said the martinet. "You know where to sit."

The boys scrambled to take their places on the stage and the martinet stepped forward to confront Moriarty and Curly. He was a short man with a prodigious chest and a hard, dry cough which he used sometimes as a nervous tic and sometimes as a form of punctuation, as when he kept the vowel short, and other times as a sort of subtext to what he was saying when he gave the vowel more mouth room.

"Brother Nestor. *Kif*. At your service. *Kof*. You wish to borrow some of my boys? *Kawf*." The last cough oozed disapproval.

"Yes." said Moriarty. "There's a dance audition next week in Ballymalloy and we wish to bring in some additional instruments, to augment the sound."

"Aah. *Kif*. Augment." This cough had a querulous tone to it, or was it a question mark?

"Yes. Make the sound bigger," Curly interjected.

"Bigger sound. *Kaf*." This was much firmer ground. "*In the Mood*? *Koof*." This was an 'I'm in control' expletive and Nestor turned to the musicians in his role as conductor.

"Right! *In the Mood. Kowf*." This was a storm cone being hoisted. "*Aon, do. Aon, do, tri*."

The augmented band started to play; the boys right on the beat, Moriarty's men a little ragged. However, as the two factions started to meld in the music, it sounded, for the first time, like real swing. The saxophones and the brass were very quickly in a solid dialogue, and the drum beats, admittedly led by the boy on the bongos, were perfectly placed. Curly was as close to ecstatic as he had ever been in Ballymalloy. He and Moriarty exchanged approving glances. Suddenly Nestor signalled a stop. His boys obeyed immediately. Moriarty's men took longer, ending raggedly, earning a disapproving glare from Nestor who turned to Moriarty and Curly.

"Well? *Kowf*." The vowel was as close to a wolf howl as the human larynx was capable of.

"I assume that all is in order?" Nestor asked. "My boys can… augment the band sufficiently?"

"I'm impressed and I think your boys are exactly right for the job," Curly admitted. "How on earth did you teach them to play swing?"

"I did not teach them to play 'swing'. *Kof.*" The vowel resonated with disapproval. "I taught them to play according to the instructions on the sheet music in front of them. They have never seen this type of music before and, *Kif*, as soon as this arrangement with Moriarty is finished, they never will again."

"I doubt it," said Curly.

Nestor's chest swelled with indignation but Moriarty butted in quickly.

"He's just taken aback with the exactness the boys show when you instruct them."

"So they should. *Kawof.*" There was no arguing with that explosion. Nestor turned to the boys.

"The national anthem," he said, raising his hand.

He signalled and the boys played the first phrase of the tune exactly and on time.

He raised his hand again and the boys stopped with instant obedience.

"Satisfied?" Nestor asked.

"Yes. Of course," said Moriarty. He looked at Curly. "We would like a clarinettist, three saxophones, two trumpets and three trombones. If that's okay with you?"

"Perfectly okay. I'll choose them and make the arrangements. Form ranks!" Nestor bellowed.

The boys hurried to obey. One of the young trombonists dropped his sheet music next to Moriarty's clarinettist and fumbled as he retrieved it, earning a *Kooof* from Nestor. The boys formed a rank in front of the stage and Nestor took his place behind them.

"*Kof!!! Anois! Do, cathar. Do, cathar. Do, cathar. Do, cathar.*"

The boys marched out and Curly looked at Moriarty.

"I must say, I'm a bit uncomfortable about using those boys," he said.

"But they're delinquents!" said the saxophone.

"Hey! Where's my flask?" said the clarinet.

Curly burst out laughing and the rest joined in.

***

Finally, the renovations in the hotel were complete. The dining room was immaculate; the stage was up and nicely decorated. Mary was helping set up the music stands, each of which sported a big, bright logo for the *Jazz* show. The sound system was installed and set up by a local hardware storeowner, who did not understand a newly discovered phenomenon called 'feedback'. That is the awkward tendency of microphone and speaker to get into each other's way, as it were. He fell into the trap of recording a sound through a microphone facing the source of the sound and then feeding it into a sound system which amplified the sound and fed it back through speakers facing the microphone. The results of this 'looping' were, in ascending order of discomfort, a rumbling, or a whining, or a whistling/screeching noise that tended to distract audiences from the show they were watching.

"My tea is hot. I can't hurry. I'll scald myself," Mrs Smith announced to the discomforted Freddie, who shrugged and headed for reception.

"We really should be going," said Mr Smith. "They have things to do here."

"That's why I'm staying," replied his spouse.

She glared at Mary, who caught the look and nipped her finger in the music stand. Into the room came the augmented band who took the places, indicated by Moriarty and Nestor. After a touch of confusion caused mainly by the underlying competitiveness of the two band leaders, they were all in place. Curly placed the gramophone on the front of the stage and Nestor moved to the centre front but was brought up short by Moriarty.

"Brother Nestor! If you please. When the boys are in my band, they are in my charge."

Nestor was taken aback but there was little he could do. Before he stepped off the stage, he stared ferociously and rattled a riff of sharp, vicious *Koffs* over them. They all stared into the middle distance. When he stepped down, the bands sorted out their instruments and their sheet music. Mrs Smith leaned towards her husband.

"They're from the reformatory, Smith," she hissed. "Watch your wallet."

"All right," Moriarty announced. "Here's the method we'll use in all rehearsals. We'll play the piece to familiarise ourselves with it. Then we'll play a record of the piece to inspire us and then we'll play the piece until I'm satisfied—"

A sharp *Kooof* stopped him.

"And until Brother Nestor is happy. *Skyliner*, by Charlie Barnet. You saxophones, nice and tight, please."

He played the piano intro and the band, led by the saxophones, took up the main theme. It sounded so good that Curly and Mary exchanged delighted grins. They played the piece to the end and Nestor approached them both and spoke in a low voice:

"I… *kof*… have to go somewhere. Brother business, you know. *Koooof.* Won't be long."

They both nodded and he disappeared with a parting glare at his boys who quailed.

They started *Peanut Vendor* on Curly's order and they played even better. Tight in the right places, looser and more jazz-like in others. The trombone player from the reform school – Johnny – suddenly broke into an Irish reel sequence in the middle. It fitted in and sounded fantastic. Moriarty was annoyed and Mary excited.

"That was *Drowsie Maggie,*" she said. "A well-known Irish reel."

"At last, some fucking improvisation," Curly said. "Okay. Let's take a break. You, second trombone. What's your name?"

"Johnny," said the gaunt teenager.

"A word with you." He and Johnny went into the bar while Mary went on to the office.

"What made you play that bit of a reel? *Drowsie Maggie,* was it?"

"Yeah. *Drowsie Maggie.* Did it work?"

"Yeah. It worked. Do you do that when Brother Nestor is around?'

"No! He'd kill me."

"Do any of the others play around like that?"

"Yeah. Three of us," Johnny said. "But not as good as me."

"Jazz?"

"No. No jazz. We never hear it. This is the first time we've seen it written down, even."

"Do you know that most jazz is improvised?"

He noted the puzzlement on Johnny's face.

"The musicians make most of it up as they go along, building on a theme. Playing what they feel like. What that sheet music does is show you the best improvisations which are put in by the band leaders. In *Peanut Vendor*, it's Stan Kenton. But the best jazz is played from the heart. Not from sheet music. What do you think of it?"

Johnny's shining face gave him the answer.

"It's great. I wish I could play it all the time."

"But the Brothers won't let you?"

"Never. We're to burn the sheet music when this is over. But I'll remember it all."

"What made you play *Drowsie Maggie?*"

"It was the right tempo. It felt the same… mood. And I wanted to… liven it up a bit while Brother Nestor wasn't there."

"What would he do if he found out?"

"Beat me. With the blackjack."

"What the hell is the blackjack?"

Johnny held his hands about eighteen inches apart.

"It's made of leather. Very hard. With bits of metal sticking through it. You'd get it on the hands. On the legs. On the... bottom until you couldn't do nothing. Couldn't hold anything. Couldn't walk. Couldn't sit."

"Jesus! For playing music?"

"For anything."

"For lessons?"

"Don't get many of them. Mostly they're the catechism. You get the blackjack for that. All the time."

"Can you read? Write?"

"No. Only music. That's hard."

Johnny winced at the memory of past lessons.

"What do you do there all day?'

"We have to go and work on the farms there. Digging potatoes, turnips, cabbages. If we work late, we have to sleep with the pigs and work again next morning."

"How long have you been there?"

"Don't know."

"Why were you sent there? Did you... do anything?"

"No. They told me my parents didn't want me so they sent me there.

As they were speaking, Johnny's face went stony and mask-like, as if hiding from the pain. Suddenly, in an abrupt change of mood, he laughed, and Curly felt shivery.

"You know what? They made us learn music as a punishment. Imagine that. A punishment." He stroked the trombone.

"Play something."

"What?"

"Anything. Play about pain."

Johnny thought a bit then placed the mouthpiece against his

lips and blew, soft and high. Out came a wail. Long and plaintive. It drifted up and down, mostly in a minor key, but then he moved the slide up and down more purposefully. The noises that came out with such force were incoherent at first, but gradually some musicality crept in which reminded Curly of the early blues that had excited him so much as a kid. Up and down the scales Johnny went, wielding the trombone like a club as if hitting the people who had – and were still – hurting him so. Blasts came out like blows to the head. Wails changed into squeaks as if in terror. But then sweet notes came, held for the longest time. The music, for now it was that, grew in volume until a triumphant series of ascending blasts ended it. The rest of the band and especially the reform boys gathered around the bar door, listening in silence. Finally, having exhausted or banished some demons within him, Johnny stopped playing and lowered the trombone. Curly said, in a tremulous voice, "That, son, is jazz. It grew out of slavery. Okay, Sergeant. More practice."

Moriarty led the boys back into the dining room and Curly went to reception where Freddie and Mary were welcoming the reporter who had arrived with his soundman in tow.

"Mr Flannigan, Miss… Erm…."

"MacBride."

"Yes. I can't believe that the big day is really, really coming."

"Yes. We're really, really excited about it and we're really glad to see you again."

"Are you really, Miss—"

"Yes. Of course." Freddie carried on with a flicker of disapproval at Mary. "Let me show you where the dancing is to take place. You can decide where you would like to be positioned."

"Thank you but I really must go and interview the townspeople. The cultural intercourse is the really, really important issue here."

"While you're here, you really must interview a Mrs Smith," said Mary. "She's the cultural custodian of Ballymalloy."

"Cultural custodian? Now that's... Thank you. Goodbye for now."

He minced out and the soundman slouched behind him.

"Cultural custodian, indeed!" Freddie exclaimed.

"Well, the cheek of him! Coming here and patronising us all. *Really!*"

Freddie and Curly exchanged amused glances. The reporter stuck his head back in.

"I forgot to ask. The band. Last time it was... well..."

"Now it's really good," said Curly.

"Really?"

"Listen," said Curly. The band was in full swing. "That's the band."

"Really?"

"REALLY!" said Freddie and Mary.

The reporter turned to go but stopped at the door, looking out into the street.

"Now that's really, really something." he gasped.

16

Nemesis

What the reporter was looking at was a spectacular young couple, both tall and slim, both with severely barbered hair, both dressed totally in black, alighting from a large black limousine with dark, dark windows. The few townspeople that were passing stopped to admire the pair, who seemed as if they had come from another planet. They were Darcy and Mitzi Powers and, as Curly had said, they were in Ballymalloy to enter the auditions, banking on the fact that the competition there would be almost non-existent and the road to Dublin and the *Jazz* show was open to them.

Darcy's grandparents, both born in Skibbereen, had emigrated to the States in the previous century, taking with them the unutterable sorrow of the Great Famine, or *an Gorta Mor* (the Great Hunger), which saw the town and its environs robbed of half its population as the potato crop failed, year after ravenous year. Unutterable though it was, the loss *was* uttered in song, poetry and story, and a hundred years later the deep-rooted anger had not abated in much of Ireland, especially in West Cork, at whose southern tip Skibbereen lay. That town produced sons and daughters with a sense of grievance, an international perspective and bone-deep contempt of so-called leaders with inflated ideas of themselves and their importance in the destiny of nations.

In 1914, the local newspaper thundered: *We give this solemn warning to Kaiser Wilhelm;* **The Skibbereen Eagle** *has its eye on you.* Darcy Powers had inherited this feeling of self-importance, a low tolerance for fools and an inexhaustible antagonism for any who stood in his way. Being graceful and athletic, he chose dancing as a career path and literally clawed his way up the ladder by means more foul than fair, which had earned him enemies and opportunities in equal numbers.

Mitzi, formerly Miriam Brice, was of Brooklyn Jewish descent and as prickly as Darcy. She had chosen dancing as a career and, thanks to her good looks and long, shapely body, had become a Rockette at the RKO Radio City Music Hall. This troupe of female precision dancers was the cynosure of 'The Showplace of the Nation' and much in demand by the endless stream of Stage Door Johnnies, as these moneyed prowlers became known. But Mitzi had kept her cool, if not her virginity, and recognised a soul and dancing mate in Darcy when they met in the *Jazz* show. They both had the firm intention of being in the new *Jazz* show and using it to strut their showy way through the cities of Western Europe.

This then, was the couple that confronted the reporter when he walked out through the hotel front door. He beckoned his soundman and stood at the top of the steps leading to the street.

"You must be contestants. I'm interested in your social intercourse with the locals while you're here. I'm from Radio Eireann."

"Radio, huh?" said Darcy. "That's cool. See my press secretary."

He jabbed his thumb over his shoulder and continued up the steps. The reporter could only see a chauffeur unloading some baggage. Freddie greeted Darcy at the door.

"Hello. I'm Freddie Flannigan, the hotel owner. Welcome to Ballymalloy."

"Yeah. It's cool to be here." Darcy took off his very dark glasses and turned to survey the street. He was not impressed. He turned back to confront Curly. They were both silent for a while.

"Darcy. Mitzi. Nice to see you."

"Wondered where you got to. Thought you were dead." Darcy stepped past him, as did Mitzi, with a cool nod. They both entered the hotel after Freddie.

***

That afternoon, Darcy and Mitzi were standing in the clear space in front of the stage in the dining room. Freddie was smoothing the French chalk onto the floorboards and testing the slipperiness. Curly and Mary were seated at the back. Darcy walked over to the box of records which stood by the gramophone on the stage. He looked through the records, selected one and walked across to where Mitzi was swaying at the edge of the space, holding it out for her inspection. She nodded in an indifferent manner and he turned to walk back, walking across the French chalk with swift, scythe-like sweepings of his long legs. Curly thought that he looked like a black venomous spider.

He placed the record on the turntable and swooped leisurely back towards the swaying Mitzi. It was *Running Wild* by Benny Goodman, and as the intro of brushes on a snare drum and clarinet began, they circled each other, picking up speed until as the theme started, they moved seamlessly into a smooth, dazzling jive. Curly hadn't seen dancing like it in years and Mary had never seen such skill.

Having magicked their way through some dazzling movements, Darcy took Mitzi by the waist and tossed her with casual ease into the air. She turned in a full circle and fell back into his waiting hands. They danced on and Curly turned and walked out the door, rubbing his ribs. Mary followed him.

Outside, Curly was muttering as he walked away.

"Jesus! He's good. Did you see those moves? Jesus!"

He stopped walking and turned to look at her.

"Maybe…"

"Maybe what!"

"Maybe I'm not good enough."

There was a long, painful pause while she summoned up all her resolve.

"Bollocks!"

Curly's jaw dropped open.

"Sure, he's good. So is she. What did you expect?" she continued. "While you hid away in Ireland, dance moved on. Got flashier. Faster. Better."

"I'll never beat him-"

"That's—"

"No. Listen. I'll never beat him. Did you see that throw? The judges will love that." He rubbed his ribs again. "I could never do that. So… we have to be different. But I don't know what new steps are out there now."

"Maybe they're not 'out there.'"

"What do you mean?'

"Remember what Johnny did on the trombone?"

"That bit of Irish music?"

"Yes. That's different."

"But Irish dancing is all so… upfuckingtight."

"I'll show you some Irish dancing that's not so uptight. More like tap."

"Where? Can *you* do it?"

"You'll see. You're going to take me on a trip this evening."

"Where to?"

"You'll see." She suddenly giggled with excitement. "I know it will work."

"What?"

"Pick me up in an hour."

167

She turned and went back into the hotel. Shaking his head, Curly followed.

***

She took him to Killorglin. Rather, she made him drive her there in the Buick. The town was on the west coast, tucked into Dingle Bay, and it was the first stop on the famed scenic road that circled the west of Kerry in its embrace. There in the shadow of the MacGillycuddy Reeks mountain range, the village was renowned far and wide for the annual Puck Fair in August. A male goat, caught on the local mountain slopes, was hoisted in a cage above the streets for the three-day duration of the fair and then released back into the wild. The festival was concerned primarily with music and dancing and secondarily with drink. The fair was scheduled for the following week, and Mary knew that plentiful rehearsals would be under way at which various styles of Irish dancing would be displayed by some of the best dancers in Ireland and, occasionally, from the Irish diaspora.

"I'm going to introduce you to my Uncle Matt. He was the one that started me dancing. He is well known throughout the country and has a very distinct style, but he insisted that I concentrated on the classical styles and wouldn't let me follow his way of dancing. But now…"

"Listen. I'm too old to learn a new style."

"No, you're not. Besides I'll be the…?"

"Focal point?"

"That's right. It'll be different and I'm sure the judges will like it."

"The only ones who will like it are Darcy and Mitzi. They'll both throw a hip out of joint laughing."

"You want something different, don't you?"

He was intimidated by her vehemence.

"Yes, but—"

"But nothing. Watch Uncle Matt but keep an open mind. Okay? Okay?"

"Okay. Okay!"

They drove through the streetscape of stone and pebble-dashed buildings, over the substantial river bridge and into the main square. Curly parked the Buick and they approached a public house in the corner. The sound of music, singing and laughter filled the evening, and an occasional cheerful group of people would move from pub to pub, laughing as they went. Occasionally, the plaintive carrying sound of the *uilleann* pipes, Ireland's major contribution to the bagpipe, emerged. The instrument was operated mainly by pressure from the elbow (*uilleann*) as the player pumped the air through the chanter. Mary got her usual shivery feeling when she heard the sound. They crossed the cobbled street and pushed their way into the pub – and into the blare of music, singing, vocal encouragement and pounding feet. Across the room, she spotted her Uncle Matt, as bulky, noisy and genial as always and, as always, surrounded by people of all ages. Mary squirmed through the crowd and into the hearty embrace that she hadn't felt for far too many years.

"Mary, a *leanabh*. You're looking gorgeous as ever. You'd think you lived on the moon, 'cause you never visit me."

"I know, Uncle Matt. I keep meaning to. This is Curly Collins. Curly, this is my favourite uncle."

Curly's hand disappeared into both of Matt's huge mitts, but the grasp was surprisingly gentle.

"Nice to meet you, Mr Collins."

"Curly, please."

"Have a drink. Both of you. Pints okay?"

"I'll have a half, Uncle Matt."

"A pint's fine with me."

"Martin, two and a half pints as quick as you like."

The formalities over, Matt put his arm around Mary.

"And what brings you all this way?"

"Dance."

"Have you taken it up again?"

"Yes. Well… the thing is, I'm entering auditions for a jazz dancing show."

"Jazz? Bejaysus!"

"And we've come for inspiration to you."

"You'll find no jazz in Killorglin. Here, get these down you."

The pints had arrived and they all sank their mouths into their respective glasses. Matt, meanwhile, never took his eyes off Mary as she took a healthy sip and wiped her mouth.

"Uncle Matt, you might find this strange, but the way you dance is very close to jazz."

She paused as he digested this, wondering if he would be in some way offended.

"My dancing is very close to many types of dancing. God gave us all two legs and when you look at it, there's a limit to the moves you can make with them. Once we stopped imitating animals in our dancing, we started to do the same basic moves. I don't suppose jazz is much different."

"But there are some of your moves that would fit into jazz so well."

"My moves?"

"I was – am – sceptical about this," said Curly. "The Irish dancing I've seen is very stiff and formal and while the footwork is very close to tap, and might indeed have inspired it, I can't see it blending in a way that the judges would appreciate."

Matt looked long and hard at Curly as he took another swallow of stout.

"Stiff and formal," he repeated. "You're right there. As I got older, I found that more and more of the energy I was putting into my dancing was diverted into keeping my hands stationery behind my hips and keeping my torso stiff as a board. Now that's fine for young dancers, and the future of classic Irish dancing is safe in their hands, but I began to lose the joy as this old body aged and it took more and more effort to move around. But the feet and the legs remained as good as ever, so I changed my style. There's many a dancing fan in this town that mocks me, but I enjoy it and it gives pleasure to many, so I keep it up."

"Is it possible that you could show me?" Curly asked.

"Sure. And this is the right place. Nobody will mind me making an eejit of myself. Tim, give us a reel there."

"Make it *Drowsie Maggie*," said Mary.

"*Drowsie Maggie* it is. Where's Fergus with that *bodhran*? This'll call for some solid rhythm."

The floor was soon cleared and Tim stepped forward with his violin and Fergus with the round, shallow Irish one-sided drum which was played with a short, double-headed stick in one hand, with the other hand altering the drum's pitch by pressing against the goatskin covering from the underside. After a slow introduction, the fiddle segued into the up-tempo reel, the bodhran took off and Matt started to move his feet to the music, slowly at first but with a quickening tempo until he was right up there with the beat. The crowd started to clap in rhythm and shout encouragement at Matt. Soon, his upper torso started to move with the music but in a loose-limbed way; his arms too started to swing, as if to counterbalance the quickening movements of his feet.

"Isn't that the tune Johnny put into *Peanut Vendor*?"

"Yes. Isn't it great?" answered Mary, her eyes shining with pride.

Curly had never seen anything like it. It reminded him of the clog dancing and the flat footing he had seen in the communities among the Appalachian Mountains, and of course the early tap dancing, but this was more graceful, and the seeming casualness of Matt's moves made it very appealing. He too started to move his feet in rhythm with Matt's and, to the crowd's enthusiastic exclamations, was soon dancing alongside him and feeling good about it. Then Mary joined in and the crowd went wild, clapping

171

and shouting. At one stage, Mary did a bicycling style of reel step as she moved, light as thistledown, across the open space, turned and danced back. It was then that Curly knew that they had a winning jive sequence. The reel ended and the three dancers returned to their pints, Matt hardly out of breath, Mary panting, and Curly exulting. This totally jazz-oriented but quintessentially Irish sequence would give their dancing at the auditions an unbeatable advantage; let Darcy gyrate as he would and let Mitzi swirl as sexily as she cared, the reel steps would conquer all.

The rest of the evening was a whirl of dancing, cheering and enthusiasm. Matt led them on a pub crawl and, in each pub, insisted on *Drowsy Maggie* and led the dancing. They soon had a loyal partisan crowd following them who whooped and cheered their three favourites to universal acclaim.

When the pubs finally closed, Matt insisted that they repair to his home, a modest cottage on the river where he lived alone. When they arrived, there were about ten men as well as Mary and Curly, and several of the men carried clinking paper bags while the fiddle player and *bodhran* players were in evidence. They both knew that their services would be required before the night ended. A fire had been damped down in the grate and Mary went to it and poked it vigorously until flames emerged. She laid on some turf sods from a blackened scuttle that stood next to the grate, and a decent fire soon started spreading its warmth around the room.

"Have you a corkscrew at all?" asked one of the men.

"Devil a one. Isn't it well known I don't drink," replied Matt as he settled himself in a high back chair facing the fire, ignoring the highly sceptical laughter. The others spread themselves around the room on various pieces of furniture. The corked bottles of stout were soon arranged in a semicircle around the fire and the men watched them with impatience. Mary went into the kitchen and scrounged around for something to eat. The fiddle player turned to Curly.

"I hear you've a well-developed larynx," he said.

"Oh yes, I can hold a tune," Curly replied.

"And what sort of a song would you be able to sing? If you were asked, that is?"

"What sort of a song would this company like to hear?"

"Do you know any Irish songs?"

"Plenty."

"Where did you learn them? In America?" asked another.

"No. In the second-best place to learn Irish songs. A Dublin pub."

"And what's the best place to sing them?"

"In a room like this full of Irishmen who've had more drinks than are good for them and are dying for the next one."

Just then, the heat of the fire made two corks pop out of their respective bottlenecks.

"Right on cue," said Matt, taking one of the bottles and handing it to Curly. "Here. Get outside of that."

"Thanks. *Slainte,* all."

He drank as the men reached for the opened bottles and placed some more next to the fire. Mary came in carrying a tray on which there were several jars containing various pickles, a selection of knives and forks, a huge loaf of bread on a board, a bread knife and a bowl of butter. Matt indicated a low stool in a corner and one of the men hastily brought it forward and placed it in front of the fire. Mary put the food on the stool and there was a moment of comfortable confusion as each man commandeered a bottle of stout and some bread and pickles fished out of the capacious jars. Mary sat on the hearth and wrapped her arms around her knees as she had done ever since she was a child. This was a time for singing and talking and reliving some of the past glories and pains of Ireland.

"We're all dying to hear a song, so what'll it be, Mr Collins?"

"Please, call me Curly."

He cleared his throat and they all were silent as he sang, in a light but true baritone, the marching song, *The Foggy Dew*. The *bodhran* player took up his drum and gave him a rhythmic accompaniment. When the song was finished, Curly received a respectful murmur of satisfaction.

"That's a good song," said Matt.

"It is," Curly agreed.

One of the men half sang and half spoke a couplet from the song, using the Irish pronunciation of the Brugha name – *Bru*. The rest murmured agreement.

"Had they died by Pearse's side, or fought with Cathal Brugha
Their bones we'd keep where the Fenian's sleep, 'neath the shroud of the foggy Dew."

Matt took up a pickled egg and held it up before his face.

"Are you patriotic at all, Curly?" he asked.

"As much as the next man," said Curly rather defensively. To be truthful, he had never before experienced such rabid patriotism as he had come across in the pubs of Dublin. It seemed that everyman had a hero in the family somewhere, and from what he had heard bandied about among the older men, every single Dubliner had been 'out' in 1916, meaning that they had played a pivotal role in the Rising that had resulted in independence for most of Ireland.

"Patriotism is like eggs," said Matt, and the men hushed, waiting for a good yarn. In the dimly lit room, the firelight etched their faces out of the darkness and on the shifting background of fire and turf and pipe smoke. "When the egg is raw, it's full of potential as a food, but it's easily broken. All it takes is heat to start it on a journey. When it's soft boiled, it's full of nutrition and has a distinctive taste that changes when it is hard boiled. And when it's pickled, like this, it's an acquired taste, not at all like the taste of a soft-boiled egg. Patriotism is an acquired taste because it very often demands uncomfortable action and that's rich on the palate. Too rich for some, dangerously rich for many."

"The MacBrides weren't slow in coming forward, were they?"

This sweetheart question gave Matt an added impetus, if, indeed, such was needed on a night of storytelling such as this.

"My family, now, the MacBrides of Mayo, have had their fair share of men who were pickled, as it were, in the injustices of the past. One of them, John MacBride, as you all know, but Curly mightn't, was executed in 1916, and his last words for the firing squad were 'I have looked down the barrels of their guns before.' And he had, in South Africa. He had taken in the hatred of the dispossessed from his father, Patrick, who had witnessed the evictions during the famine, and that guided him for the rest of his life, and when John MacBride met the woman he was to marry, Maude Gonne, she had also inherited, from her mother Edith Gonne, the burning sense of injustice at the brutal treatment of the Irish during the Great Hunger, when what wheat there was growing in the land was sent to England while the Irish starved in their millions.

"The original Gonne family, do you see, had a large house and property in Mayo, and Edith, although she lived in England and France, spent much of the year there and was fluent in Irish. During the famine, the farm was guarded by a troop of English dragoons while the harvest was being taken in, even as the starving Irishmen and women were passing on their way to the coast and, maybe, a ship to your country, Curly. When the two of them got together, heavy with their hatred, they were highly combustible. She was a firebrand, that one."

"It was said that she was worth a battalion in the Rising," said one of the men while Matt wet his mouthful of egg with a drink of porter.

"She was. She was indeed, especially when Willie Yates wrote some rousing parts for her on the stage," Matt agreed, as he swallowed the egg and porter. "Let me tell you about the experiences of both their parents, which, instilled into them with their mothers' milk, brought them together with one burning intention – to free Ireland."

To say Curly was interested was a gross understatement. Not since his evening with Rathbone had he been so immersed in history-telling. He was beginning to think that Ireland was full of master storytellers who had total command of their history and who could bring it to vibrant, fascinating life. He was particularly taken with the MacBride and Gonne saga, how their paths had crossed and how MacBride had been swept up in the national adulation of Maude Gonne. He had known vaguely about their love affair, but he did not understand the grip such a woman could have on the imagination of a nation. There had been women in American history who had influenced events through their beauty, their cleverness or their positions of power, but none who could become the focus of nationalistic fervour. He was totally taken with the sheer romance of Gonne and Yeats and MacBride that he felt he just had to know more about it. So, when the men in Matt's home had departed one by one and quietly and Mary had slumped into deep sleep on the couch, he opened one of the last bottles of stout and offered it to Matt, who was still wide awake and lost in his thoughts of an Ireland that was rich in great and moving stories.

"Tell me more about Maude and Yeats," he said. "They seem to embody the entire spirit of rebellion that brought the Rising about. We have great stories about the American War of Independence but there are no women in them, even though they must have been there, inspiring their men to great deeds. No Maude Gonne. No Willie Yeats carrying the flames, ready to be lit."

"I'm sure there must have been such women," Matt mused as he sipped at the stout.

"Oh yes. I remember one. From the Civil War. I used to love it at school because it was the only poem they tried to teach me that had a real story in it and great rhymes that you couldn't forget. It's about a Unionist woman, ninety years old she was, who defied Stonewall Jackson's Confederate troops as they marched through her home town. She waved a Union flag out the window…

'Shoot if you must this old grey head,
But spare your country's flag' she said.'"

"Barbara Frietchie was her name," said Matt.

"How the hell do you know that?"

"Because good poems, like good wines, travel well. Go on. There's another great thumping rhyme at the end of that verse."

Curly collected his thoughts and recited:

"'A shade of sadness, a blush of shame,
Over the face of the leader came;
The nobler nature within him stirred
To life at that woman's deed and word...'"

To his surprise, Matt joined in, thumping the arms of his chair as they both bellowed out the final couplet.

"'Who touches a hair of yon gray head
Dies like a dog! March on!" he said.'"

They both looked at each other with delighted satisfaction.

"See? There's always a woman involved in great events, even though they don't usually get the recognition they deserve," said Matt finally. "But in our story, there never was such an explosive mixture of national rapture and unrequited love in two people that enthralled and inspired a nation." Matt mused. "Yeats wrote stage roles that ignited intense emotion in the nation. Especially among Dubliners, and Gonne presented them in a manner that drove them mad. But one play, *The Countess Kathleen,* had them totally divided. And to add to it all, there was George Moore, a writer and novelist. He was also from Mayo where his father was a very fair landlord, but that didn't stop the republicans burning down the Moore family home in the 1920s. You see, there was a lot of anger all over Ireland, especially among the writers and artists, about the injustices of the invaders as well as the effect a stifling religion had on the people. Both our families, and their baggage, were part and parcel of it all, so when the two families came together, at the marriage of Maude Gonne and John MacBride, how could the marriage possibly last? He was blinded by her patriotic image from the first and she by his warrior image when she realised what he could do for the cause. It turned out a disaster. For both of them."

Curly was mesmerised at the picture he was drawing of a pre-Rising Dublin and its denizens, and they both gazed sleepily at the fire as it collapsed in soft cascades. The time for talk was over for the night.

17

The auditions

The next morning, Mary and Curly set off for Joy's house for more practising. Curly was strangely silent.

"Well, how did you enjoy last night?" she asked.

"Very much. Both the dancing – especially yours and Matt's – and Matt's storytelling. I was fascinated."

"He's a national treasure, Uncle Matt. He says his first duty is to make sure the MacBride family knows their history. That's why he tells those stories. I grew up on them."

"And how do you feel about it all?"

"About all the history? I'm… not sure. I'd never tell Uncle Matt but it's all over, you know. It's a new Ireland and we've sorted out nearly all the problems. One thing is for sure, we'll never allow such oppression again."

"Somebody once said that 'eternal vigilance is the price of liberty.'"

"And what have we to be vigilant about? Aren't we a free people? And one thing – we'll never be oppressed again."

"How do you know?"

"Haven't we good people looking after us?"

"People like who?"

"Father O'Grady, for one. And the Church behind him. It would never let such… things happen, ever again. Anyway, Mr Collins, has America got the exclusive secret to peaceful living?"

"No. I don't think so. I just—"

"Well, then. I'm happy that we have such a good life. Look at the jail! Who's in there? Only old Dermot who goes in there once a month to dry out. And Sergeant Moriarty keeps 'eternal vigilance' over him – like an old hen."

Curly knew it was time to 'button his lip'.

"Sorry, Mary. I was just… intrigued. In the States, it took a very long time for the anger to die down after independence, and here in Ireland, it's only, what, thirty years since you got your freedom, and all over I see or hear about English people still living well and being involved in running things. It's remarkable."

Mary was immediately mollified.

"Except when blow-ins like you come over and think you can teach us how to dance. The cheek of you! You only started to walk upright when you had killed all the buffaloes."

And she linked her arm in his. Stunned by her logic, Curly held his peace.

Back in Joy's living room, he put *Peanut Vendor* on the gramophone and holding Mary's hands loosely he talked his way through the number, working out the approach.

"Darcy is good, very flashy and confident. Maybe that's his weak spot. They probably have hundreds of moves and sequences, rehearsed again and again until they're second nature and maybe that's another weakness. Whatever the music, they can go with it. They think as one and once he, or she, starts a move, the other understands and goes with it. Well, that may be okay for a small-town audition but not for a small-town audition with Curly and MacBride. Hey, that's not a bad name for a dancing duo."

She laughed dismissively but he went on probing the music, half dancing, half improvising, but he was seeking a place to insert their reel sequence. This meant listening to the piece several times, trying various parts of it and working out a proper sequence.

Two hours went by and she was very impressed by his powers of concentration and, already familiar with the music, she had absorbed it totally until she knew it intimately. Finally, she stopped suddenly.

"Listen. I need a break. A cup of tea and some fresh air."

He was immediately apologetic.

"I'm sorry, Mary. Yeah, let's take a break."

He walked out into the street and walked up and down, thinking hard and humming the music under his breath. Soon, Mary came out holding two cups of tea. They stood a while in thought and then, after a few sips, he spoke softly but intensely.

"We have to work out the sequence and we have to dance it twice. The first time to excite the judges and the crowd and then, when they are begging for more, we do it again. That means choosing the exact spots and structuring the steps around and into them."

She suddenly had a worrying thought.

"What if they give us some other music to dance to?"

"No, they won't. Here's how these auditions work. They narrow the couples down to the most accomplished – and the most popular – so they watch the audience closely. They're looking for audience appeal."

He stopped and looked Mary up and down critically.

"Well? What are you thinking?"

"I'm thinking that you'll beat Mitzi hands down in the popularity stakes. She's great but too cool. A bit distant. Uninvolved. Too flashy. You're real. Fresher. You have an air of country innocence about you."

"Thanks. You're saying I'm a *culchie*."

"What the hell is a *culchie*?"

"It's a very common name for a country... what's the word?"

"Bumpkin."

"A country bumpkin. It's an insulting name given to a country person by Dubliners. It comes out of the name for Kiltimagh, a little town in Mayo."

"*Culchie* MacBride. It could catch on."

She gave him a thump.

"You were saying about the choice of music."

"I was. The judges choose the music for the mixed couples, but then each of the highest scoring couples do a final dance to music of their own choice. That's when we choose *Peanut Vendor* and win."

"Won't Darcy try to do better?"

"No. He's too arrogant because he's so good. His weak spot is that he can't imagine anyone in Ballymalloy near good enough to challenge him, least of all a has-been like Curly Collins. His 'better' is his best. We'll keep our choice of music a secret, but even if he does find out, he won't be able to beat us."

"Promise?"

"Mary! I'm too old to promise anything. But I seriously believe we have a good chance of winning and of getting you to Dublin."

"Aren't you interested in going to Dublin too?"

It was a while before he answered.

"No."

"Then why are you doing this? And don't say 'for me' because I don't feel like crying right now."

It was another while before he sorted out his thoughts.

"For both of us. For you primarily because... well, because. But for me; because dancing has given me a good life and I think it will give you the same. It's a sort of rite of passage."

"That's supposed to be for me to go through."

"For me too."

They looked at each other as Mary blinked back her tears, and the embrace that the occasion demanded was so comforting that Curly, the consummate seducer, felt, not excited by it but enriched. It wasn't a feeling he was used to.

***

During the practice that evening, all the thought he had put into the final dance coalesced into a clear and coherent sequence of moves.

"First off, we have to do that throw of his. Early, not saving it for a great finale as he will, but almost as a throwaway. We'll steal his thunder."

"Can you do it? You're sore there." She stroked his lower ribs. "What happened anyway? How did it get sore?"

"I… er… I hurt it at the factory. Slipped and fell. Silly really."

He flushed slightly as he remembered Freddie's anguished anger at his desecration of Mary. Mary knew there was some deep reason for those sore ribs, but she also knew that it was forbidden territory.

"Do you want to try it now?"

"I'll have to, won't I?"

"To music?"

"Music will help."

He put on *Peanut Vendor* and walked through the intro and the trombone insertions.

"There. There. Where the trombone plays the longer riff. That's where we'll do the throw, and then we'll move on as if it had never happened. Okay?"

She nodded and stepped up to him. They jived to the Cuban rhythm of the introduction, and as the trombone let loose, he caught her and threw her up into the air. She turned a full thirty-six degrees and fell back into his waiting hands in total trust. He caught her and his breath, but he knew that he could do it in the final.

"Good," he said. "Let's plot the rest. We—"

"You okay?"

"Yes. Yes. Now let's find the place for your little reel steps."

They played the rest of the number and the place for the routine was where he had suspected it would be; where the dissonance came with the brass. The first time it swung and that's where he put it. She did her bicycling steps away from him and he moved in a wide circle around her to pick her up again as she finished the steps. The second time for the routine was when the trombones and trumpets were really at each other's throats, and this time she made her move slightly bigger, again for the third dissonance, and at the fourth blast, he grabbed her with a passion and threw her up into the air. She fell back into his hands and dropped softly but firmly onto the floor on the final beat of the music. They were grinning idiotically at each other, knowing that they had a winning sequence.

***

The influx of a large crowd into a heretofore quiet town is traumatic. When all available rooms in the town and all available beds in the neighbourhood are let for rates ranging from the exorbitant to the ridiculous, then all residual and instinctive feelings of hospitality are virtually extinguished. Everybody who came for the auditions for the *Jazz* show; producers, dancers, judges, organisers and hangers-on were perceived as legitimate targets for exploitation. In the minds of those denizens of Ballymalloy who existed on a level barely above actual penury, the unexpected short-term influx of funds opened up dreams of increased income that stretched way, way into the future.

There was talk, among those with space to let, of annual auditions, of the *Jazz* show being staged every year and in the vicinity, of visitors who would be so taken with the attractions of Ballymalloy that they would relocate there. An unofficial gathering of townsfolk even planned a publicity campaign for the town. A whiff of additional income (not yet paid) generated plans of astounding ambition and firm intentions of expanding existing accommodation to an astronomical level. So, the cost of basic goods and foodstuffs increased way beyond the reach of the locals – to the detriment of all. Everybody's energy levels increased as houses were decorated, old cars given air in their tyres for the first time in years, carts and traps, long past serviceable condition, were patched up and painted, and horses and donkeys, long left out to pasture, were crammed back into harness, much to the animals' distress.

So, the town awaited the arrival of the event. There were a few sceptics who didn't believe in the honesty of auditions, the actuality of the *Jazz* show, the morals of the dancers, the impartiality of the judges or the desirability of jazz dancing as a whole. But they were in the minority because they could not see any possibility of themselves benefitting, in any form, from the event.

The Ballymalloy Hotel was the immediate and prime beneficiary, with pre-bookings, deposits and an assured increase in business, and Freddie had invested in advertising in the local and trade press which he thought had a fair chance of building future business. He had a supply of colour leaflets printed and had sent them to the national tourist board, *Bord Failte*, for inclusion in their sporadic mailings. His expectations were, at least, grounded on sound business principles. The increasing absence of Mary from her hotel duties inconvenienced him but did not perturb him. He had loved her silently and discreetly for many years, but he was as excited as she at the possibility of her getting to Dublin and starting a new career.

On the first day of the auditions, the tumult was considerable. Busloads of contestants arrived throughout the morning. Impressive-looking cars offloaded judges and officials. Cartloads of flowers disgorged their fragrant and colourful loads, and the band had assembled on the raised balcony across the road from the hotel. They diligently practised their appointed numbers and since, by now, the policemen among them had gained considerable confidence, there was less alcohol consumed. They were very at home with the chosen repertoire of jazz numbers, and the clarinettist had had his teeth glued more securely. Moriarty had adopted the poise and mannerisms of Duke Ellington, whom he had seen in a film, and he intro'd the numbers and apportioned the solos with consummate aplomb. They were swinging their way through *The Woodchoppers' Ball* on the raised pavement in front of the hotel balcony when two very inebriated locals set out across the street towards the band. A bus screeched to a stop inches away from flattening them. The driver sat on his horn and screamed obscenities. One of the drunks pulled himself erect and waved airily at the driver.

"Ah, would you ever cop on. What else did you get for Christmas?"

They both reached the other side of the road and paused to admire the band.

"Is that hard to play?" one asked, prompting the other to finish the old chestnut.

"Because it's fecking hard to listen to," obliged the other. Twisting and squirming at their own devastating humour, they staggered on towards the next pub.

On the raised pavement, under an old twisted oak tree a few yards from the hotel, a bookie had set up his stall and a bookie's blackboard on a metal stand. On it he had written all the contestants' names.

"Place your bets, ladies and gentlemen. Place your bets. The Powers is the favourite couple. Generous odds on your particular fancy. Place your bets."

Artie shouldered his way through the crowd.

"Ten pounds on Mary MacBride and Curly Collins."

"Will you look at that, people. Here's a local man betting

heavily on a local couple. Long odds on them, like the rest of the board – 20 to 1. Are you still game?"

"What's the odds on the Powers?" another punter asked.

"The Powers is 8 to 1," the bookie explained.

"That short?"

"That short. They're the hot favourites. He's the brightest star of New York, so he is."

"I'm still game," Artie persisted, holding out his ten pounds.

"That's a darling punter. Ten pounds on Curly and Mary it is – at 20 to 1."

He scribbled the details on a slip and swopped it for Artie's ten pounds. Artie tucked the slip into an inside pocket and made his way towards the hotel car park. There he approached the Buick, next to which Curly was standing, admiring his reflection in the gleaming bodywork. He looked up as Artie approached.

"Artie, you're wasted on this town," he said as he stroked the place which Artie had repaired.

"It's a pity about the ornament."

"No, it's not. It makes the Buick look like a bandit."

"A bit like you."

"A bit like me. Do I owe you anything?"

"No. It was great to make that American car look like new. I defy what's his name, Ford, to do any better."

"You're right there. Now, one more thing."

He hands the groaning Artie his car keys.

"My bag's in my room and the box of records. Please get them when the dancing starts and put them in the trunk and leave the keys under the seat. Okay?"

"Okay. But what about the gramophone?"

"My bequest to the great and glorious town of Ballymalloy and all who live in her. Artie, I owe you."

"Yes, you do," said the long-suffering Artie, but when Curly walked back into the hotel, the look Artie threw after him was full of admiration – and envy.

"Just make sure Mary wins," he called after him, but all he got was a jaunty wave of the hand.

Father O'Grady was on the street too, admiring the crowd as he pushed Joy along the heaving sidewalk.

"Wouldn't it be great if a praying contest could get such a crowd?" he said as they reached the steps up to the hotel.

"Excuse me, please," said Joy.

With the casual courtliness of the Irish working class, the crowd parted and many hands hoisted the wheelchair and Joy up the steps.

"Let us do it, Father."

"There you are, Missis."

"Show them how to do the waltz, Miss Joy."

"I'll bet you could have danced rings round them all."

Laughing, Joy riposted, "*Go raibh mait agat.* Thanks to you all. They wouldn't know what a waltz is. I could have too, danced rings around them. Not so long ago either."

And so, she and Father O'Grady were deposited in the hotel with respect.

Not so Mrs Smith and the Abelard to her Heloise, Mr Smith. She had donned her finest bib and tucker, which, being of considerable age and inappropriateness, made her, the feigned lamb, look decidedly like the proverbial mutton. Mr Smith, in a very tight and uncomfortable dress suit and badly tied white tie, wallowed in her ample wake. The locals couldn't resist the *lese majesty.*

"Ten to one on the ould wan."

"I'll wait until she does the jitterbug before I back her."

"If she can jitter, I'm a bug."

Mrs Smith, usually disdainful of such plebeian barbs, was considerably ruffled, and Mr Smith suffered martyrdom as he passed. On gaining the relative safety of the hotel reception, she paused to adjust her bib, tucker and equilibrium and was calming herself when she was confronted by a microphone thrust into her face as the reporter asked:

"As the local cultural custodian of Ballymalloy, Mrs… erm…"

"Smith."

"Yes… Smith; would you like to comment on the social intercourse that is taking place between the contestants and the local population?"

"Smith," said Mrs Smith icily, "are you going to let me be insulted like that?"

Mr Smith's doubtless enraged reaction was stifled by the increased commotion of the sombre group of judges, led by the beetle-browed chairman and ushered in by a flustered Freddie. Curly came into reception with Mary to view the judges. He blanched as he caught sight of a tall and particularly flinty-eyed tanned man among them. Mary caught his expression as he turned away.

"What?"

"That tall guy. He threw me out of an audition for the first *Jazz* show. Jesus! I hope he doesn't recognise me. And we're using the same music. Jesus!"

"Mr – Curly, that was years ago. He won't recognise you and even if he does, he—"

"You don't know these producers! They spit fucking rivets. They're as hard-hearted a bunch of bastards as ever shat between two shoes."

Mary was quite shocked at his language but realised that this wasn't the time for squeamishness.

"Get over it! What are you going to do? Dance in a mask? Run out the back? Just don't look at him in the dancing. Concentrate on the chairman. He looks… I don't know… benign."

"This is show business. There's no room for 'benign' in show business."

"There's no room for nerves either. Is there?"

He looked at her long and hard but gradually, the smile crept in and he shrugged sheepishly.

"You're right. I'm acting like an amateur. Sorry."

"The dance, Curly, nothing but the dance. Come on, let's run through the final routine again."

They drifted off into a back room to practise. Again.

18
Joy

The auditions went as auditions usually go. There were conflicting objectives among the judges. Some – mainly Irish – judges saw the auditions as a genuine outreach programme, empowering and encouraging local dancers and willing to take a chance with some contestants. Others – principally the New York producer – were looking for talent that was uniquely good and were prepared to be brutal with mediocrity. The chairman was a producer of the show *and* one of the main sponsors, and he wanted to loosen if not break the hold that East Coast dancers and promoters had on the international dancing scene. However, they had several things in common which boded well for the project: they acknowledged the valuable publicity the auditions would generate, they sincerely loved dancing and they all knew their jobs.

To the townspeople of Ballymalloy, the auditions were a matter of national, county, barony, parish and town pride, perhaps retribution, maybe even revenge. And which nation on the planet has not got a never-to-be-forgotten national or tribal slight for which blood, or at least imprecations and tears, should be shed? The ingress of the Yankee dancers and the factionalism of the auditions occasioned well-lubricated reminiscences in the various Ballymalloy pubs about the ancient battles of Ireland, such as Moy Tura, the war between the *Tuatha de Danann* and the *Fir Bolg* (the Bag Men) in prehistoric times. The latter lost and were banished to Greece, where they were forced to carry bags of earth to enrich a barren plain on which they were forcibly settled. The former took over Ireland until the Celts came, with whom they shared the land; all above ground to the Celts, all below to the Danann who, out of spite, became the source of faerie. These ancient battles were, in the overwrought collective memories of the Irish, fought by opposing armies of Bronze Age Charles Atlases in furs, carbuncles and colourful cloaks. Brian Boru, Ireland's last high king, was recalled, and his victory over the Vikings celebrated again and again.

On a more contemporary and local level, the age-old enmity between Cork and Tipperary was resuscitated with lusty renderings of the song about the Cork hurler, the *Bould Tady Quill*, who beat the bejazus out of the Tipperary team. All in all, to these latter-day misunderstood martyrs, it was retribution time. Time to reclaim the honour of the ancient Gaels, if necessary, to the last dance. Patriotism reigned, hearts beat high and maudlin memories of former glory days abounded.

Meantime, in the packed arena where these mighty issues were being resolved, the stage was barely adequate for the band and the judges, while the considerable crowd was accommodated by three rows of chairs around the three sides of the room, with standing room behind them. The dancers congregated in the lounge and the reception, all of which opened onto the dining room, and they peered in to watch proceedings. The opening stages were relatively easy to manage and agreed upon. The dancers were allowed on the floor, four pairs at a time, and the talented were easily identified, even though the better ones were taking no chances and the lacklustre were easily eliminated. As the field narrowed, the dancers were given floor space two pairs at a time and the standard of dancing improved progressively. The excitement among the crowd grew appreciably and runners were in action, taking bets out to the bookie, who had sneaked into reception. When the field narrowed to the final four couples, the tension was almost unbearable. It was clear that the cleavage lines were between Curly and Mary and Darcy and Mitzi. The odds given by the bookie backed this up, as did the vehemence of the drum roll which introduced the couples as they were called forward.

When the first couple, from down Cork way, was called forward, the drummer gave a perfunctory roll on the drums, slightly condemnatory of the Southerners with the sign-song accent. The second couple, from Mallow, received a roll that showed a modicum of partisanship insofar as being the closer location to Ballymalloy and the fact that the area produced a highly-appreciated red cheese merited a rattling cymbal crash at the end. Darcy and Mitzi received more cymbal than drum, a clear indicator of the scepticism of the crowd as to Darcy's actual right to be a participant; a 'blow-in' was subtly indicated to percussive aficionados and "her skirt is too tight' was clearly signalled by the disapproving dampening of the double-cymbal high hat. But the local favourite, Mary, in spite of her handsome but slightly suspect partner, called forth an extended drum roll on the snare drum which was augmented by a 'shave-and-a-haircut-two-bits' (in Ireland, it's 'how-is-your-ould-wan? Game-ball') sequence on the bass drum and an unanswerable battering of the cymbal and the undampened high hat. A share of the resounding applause was directed at the drummer by those in the crowd who understood such auditory comments, and when the chairman signalled him to stop, he raised his arms and rattled his sticks together in appreciation of the crowd's acknowledgement of his skill.

The number chosen by the judges for the four couples was *Running Wild* and the speed of the piece set a high standard from the opening brushwork solo. This soon proved too much for the Cork and Mallow couples who seemed to lag behind the beat. In fact, they were lagging behind Curly and Darcy who both had that instinctive anticipation of the dramatic beats that makes excellent dancing seem to draw drama out of the music rather than a passive acceptance of the tempo set by the band. The difference in the dancing was such that the couple from Cork were totally discouraged and dropped out of the competition and slowly walked off the floor. The Mallow couple decided to brave it out, but they restricted themselves to a small part of the floor, in obvious deference to the others.

Darcy had the bit between his teeth and his animosity was palpable. On one fast, whirling traverse of the floor towards Curly and Mary, he spun Mitzi at his full reach and so many times that her momentum, increasingly affected by the acceleration which Darcy imposed on her body, increased dramatically. Darcy deliberately set her on a collision course with Mary, who was also spinning at the end of Curly's arm. Newton's third law of motion was about to be demonstrated as an impact became imminent. Mary's body, if hit by Mitzi's fast moving one, would exert an equal force on Mitzi in the opposite direction. The effect on their limbs and organs would have been disastrous had not Curly snatched Mary out of the way in the nick of time. In her chair at the front of the crowd, Joy caught her breath and pressed her hand on her breast. Always a pale woman, her face went whiter than ever. She looked at the priest but he was watching the dancers.

In his fury at Darcy's irresponsibility, Curly almost lost control of Mary. Darcy's grin of derision was an added goad to his rage. When the number was brought to a speedy if messy end by Moriarty, the two men had to be restrained by their partners; Curly wanting to attack Darcy and Darcy moving forward as if welcoming conflict. The audience was divided; some were angry at such recklessness, others were excited by this increase in the stakes. The judges conferred briefly and the chairman beckoned Darcy forward. From Darcy's frozen face, it was clear that a warning was being issued and that Darcy was forced to accept it if he wanted to continue.

Having dismissed Darcy, the chairman signalled to the drummer who obliged with a loud drum roll.

"Ladies and gentlemen," he announced and waited until the noise faded. "Mr Darcy Power has been given a warning that any such further irresponsible behaviour will result in instant disqualification. Now there will be a ten-minute break until the leading two couples face each other in the final to music of their own choice. They are Mr Collins and Miss MacBride (loud applause) and Mr and Mrs Power (equally loud applause)."

The band started to play *In The Mood,* and the crowd loosened and some made for the bar for a well-earned drink. Father O'Grady pushed Joy towards the reception and some of the fresh air that was finding its way through the open door.

"Did you ever see such exciting dancing?" he asked her.

She smiled quietly.

"Oh yes."

The priest smiled back at her and turned to look out into the street, so he didn't see her catch her breath again, and again press her hand to her breast for a longer time than before. The street was still buzzing, the bookie still taking in bets and the odds were very short on both couples. Artie slide over to him and waved his slip with its 20 to 1 odds on it. The bookie scowled at him but Artie smiled and headed back into the hotel. The reporter was still functioning and the badly jostled soundman was doing his best to record it all:

"A moment ago," he said, "the crowd was gasping at the speed and dexterity of the last two couples. A really, really, dangerous move by one of the couples came close to causing a really bad accident. But the couple has been warned that they will be disqualified if such a thing happens again. And now two dances remain. Each to the individual couples' choice of music. I must say that, although it has been very exciting to witness the contest on the dance floor of this, the premier, in fact the only hotel in Ballymalloy, I am rather surprised that the social intercourse was unremarkable. In fact, not to put too fine a point on it, there was none that I could see. The dancers came, they danced and they went away. But perhaps that is due to the reticence of the locals here in West Cork. However, I will return to the hotel and bear witness to the final… confrontation on the dance floor."

At the entrance to the dining room, Brother Nestor slid past Curly as he made for the street.

"Have to go somewhere for a while. Brother business."

Curly looked after him with disinterest.

This was the penultimate dance and both Curly and Darcy had independently decided to up the stakes. There would be no quarter given. Each couple would dance to the uttermost of their ability, each person in the whole of their health and their bodies in peak condition. Neither couple would have the other to measure themselves against and to fine-tune their moves in response to some legerdemain by the other. Darcy had chosen *Sing, Sing, Sing* as their last number and had worked out a much more sophisticated routine now that they were going toe to toe with Curly and Mary. As Moriarty started to count the band in, Mary, who was standing with Curly at the lounge doorway, looked around for Joy, but there was no sign of her, or of the priest.

"Where's Joy?" she asked Curly but he shook his head impatiently and concentrated on the dancing. As the tom-tom intro started, Darcy and Mitzi started a low-down and snake-like routine, bodies almost bent double, feet moving in intricate steps that were difficult to follow, so fast were they. As the trombones and trumpets started a dialogue, they started to come erect, and as the main theme with the entire band began, Darcy did his throwing act; Mitzi spun and fell back down into his hands and he planted her on the floor. The crowd roared at the move and the couple was off on a blistering and complex dance. This was no unconnected series of moves; this was a complete and carefully rehearsed routine from start to finish. The two had obviously studied the number with care and interpreted it with ingenuity. Curly looked at them aghast; they were magnificent. This was realms above what they had been dancing before, and the crowd loved it, whistling, clapping and stomping their feet in appreciation and awe. Mary, however, watched the throw, faultlessly delivered, which scared her, waited for the subsequent routine and then looked around for Joy. Instead, she saw Father O'Grady beckoning her. She slipped away from Curly and hurried over to join him.

Mr Smith, who had been gazing at the dancers, enthralled, heard his spouse say:

"I really don't know what they're making all this fuss about."

Forty years of resentful submission flavoured his reply.

"Oh, do be quiet for once in your life."

Her jaw dropped as she stared at him.

Drawing Mary out of the dining room and towards the office, the priest looked at her gravely.

"It's Joy. She got a shock at that near collision and her heart..."

Mary rushed into the study to see Joy stretched out on the couch, with the priest's housekeeper in attendance, holding one of Joy's hands and mopping her forehead. She looked up and exchanged resigned glances with the priest. Mary threw herself on her knees beside Joy, and holding her hand in both of hers she leaned forward to rest her cheek against Joy's. Joy mumbled something and Mary placed her ear against the pale lips onto which her tears fell.

"What? Auntie Joy? What?" she whispered and leaned closer as Joy breathed one word.

"Dublin" was the word.

"Yes, Auntie Joy. Dublin. For you."

Father O'Grady started to mutter in a low but distinct voice.

"In sure and certain hope of the resurrection to eternal life through Our Lord Jesus Christ..."

The housekeeper reached back and drew Smack out of the corner and pushed him gently to his knees next to Joy. Joy looked at him and a beatific smile lit up her face.

"Joe," she whispered. "Joe. I never thought I'd see you again."

Through her tears, Mary looked at Smack and for the very first time saw the likeness between Smack and Joy who, at that moment, exhaled quietly and expired.

"The Lord bless her and keep her. The Lord make His Face to shine upon her..."

The music from the dining room stopped amidst loud and prolonged applause and cheers. Curly rushed into the room and understood the situation. He crossed to the couch, bent down and kissed the gracious old lady goodbye.

"Dublin," said Mary through her sobs. "She said Dublin."

Curly softly and gently took her hand.

"Then let's do this for Joy," he said.

Mary stifled a sob, wiped her eyes and rose to her feet.

"Let's," she said as she allowed Curly to lead her back into the dining room.

19

The final

This was a dance for Joy de Burg, a celebration of a life of dancing cut short by a terrible fall and a dancing life cut short by the grim reaper himself. Mary and Curly were so emotional and tightly strung as they faced each other waiting for the music to begin that they were in a highly receptive mood to the raw, pounding amalgam of the Cuban rhythm and sassy, brassy East Coast swing of *Peanut Vendor*.

Long ago, Curly had imagined the number as the quintessence of the jazz story, but his perceptions had changed since then, as had his emotional needs. Now he was dancing for Joy who had lost a love and a skill at the same time and for Mary whom he had betrayed. So, the dance was one of remembrance and atonement. He knew he would never go to Dublin and get involved in the hurly-burly of professional dancing ever again but he would get Mary there or die trying. His ambition regarding the upcoming dance was to make it a chronicle of dance itself, from the intoxicating Caribbean rhythms which incorporated old European elements infused into Spanish music, and music forms brought from West Africa and the Congo by black slaves and then incorporated into the jazz corpus where it evolved into the swing, bop and jive phenomena, inspiring some of the most creative musicians in the world. Also, the sequence they had devised from the Irish reel played a major role in the story. To him it represented all the graceful rural foot pounding of the Gaelic world, its antecedents in Eastern Europe and its off-shoots across the Atlantic. And the full-blown swing resolution in the middle and the end epitomised the explosion of American jazz onto the world stages and dance floors. Truly, the great American Art Form.

To Mary, the upcoming dance represented, first of all, her personal tribute to the woman who had shaped most of her life through kindness, generosity of spirit and an underlying adamantine honesty which could shock and illuminate at the same time. It was also a form of benediction to the man who, irrespective of his reasons – redemption being one of them – had taken the modicum of dancing skill she had and elevated it to a level from where she could attempt ingress into the international world of dance. A trip to Dublin, she knew, was merely the first in a long series of steps to a professional career, but it was the crucial step which, if not taken, would condemn her to a life of obscurity and plaintive musing on what might have been. The Irish reel sequence, which she had introduced and helped perfect, outclassed anything she had seen from Darcy and Mitzi, and she had implicit trust in the story of dance with which Curly had imbued the music. If Darcy represented the state of international jazz dancing out there, then she knew, in her bones, that what she and Curly had devised was something unique and, if she gave it all she had, something better.

Their dance was a sensation that had the crowd shouting and the judges grinning at each other. Even the flinty-eyed tanned producer was returning the chairman's smiles and nodding. Into the twenty-second bongo and guitar intro, they threw a creative amalgam of various Cuban and African steps, simple but highly evocative of indigenous rhythms. The first throw-up into the air and graceful landing on the trombone riff brought a full-throated roar of approval. But when Johnny played the *Drowsie Maggie* bars and when Mary did the Irish reel bicycling steps across the floor, lightly and airily, towards the smoothly circling Curly, the cheering almost drowned out the music. One reel had the crowd totally on their side, two had them fervent proselytes, and the final throw and the landing precisely on the last note of music elicited the roar of the totally converted. Curly's ribs were on fire but he staunchly refused to hold or to rub them. The judges rose to their feet as one, and the tanned producer was no longer flinty-eyed.

The band started to play *American Patrol* and most of the crowd started to dance, some even trying to jive, with remarkable lack of success. Mr Smith eyed his still angry soulmate.

"Would you care to dance, my dear?"

She looked long and hard at him and sighed.

"I suppose so. But I refuse to do any of that jitter-smitter."

"Wouldn't dream of asking you, my dear."

They stood up and started a very tentative foxtrot.

The dance was stopped halfway through by the chairman, who stepped up onto the stage and signalled Moriarty, who signalled the drummer, who stopped the rest of the band and brought the dancers to a stop with the most movement-inhibiting drum roll ever played, culminating in a smash on the cymbals.

"Ladies and gentlemen, that brings an end to the auditions in the lovely town of… er…"

"Ballymalloy!" bellowed the crowd in one voice.

"Ballymalloy," the chairman agreed. "The couple who—"

"Which," interjected Moriarty.

"Which…" agreed the chairman, "… will proceed to Dublin for a final audition for the wonderful show – *Jazz* – is… are…" A tentative glance at Moriarty. "Is…" Another glance "…comprised of Curly Collins and Mary MacBride." A roar of agreement greeted his choice if not his grammar. "We, us judges, will now proceed to County Clare—"

The crowd, imbued with local pride and enthusiasm, booed loudly.

"… Killaloe for the last of the auditions and then return to Dublin with the recommended participants in the final selection. And now, goodnight, Ballymalloy."

He referred to a note which he took from his pocket.

"*Slan leat.*"

"*Slan libh,*" yelled the crowd.

"Okay, okay. *Slean libh.*"

"*Slan leat,*" yelled the crowd.

The chairman turned to a fellow judge in puzzlement.

"But that's what I said."

"You say *libh* when you're saying goodbye to many people, *leat* when you're saying it to one person. They were replying to you," said the fellow judge.

"Christ! Nothing's easy in this country."

"No. It's not," yelled the crowd as it broke up in laughter.

In the lounge, Darcy and Mitzi were gathering their things for departure. He was furious and she was her usual unperturbable self.

"Where the hell did they get that routine? I've never seen it before," he snarled.

"That's why the judges liked it."

"Christ! A bit of Irish bog-trotting. Anyone can do that."

"Yeah. Now that they've seen it."

"Hey. You could do it as well as her."

"Yeah, I could, but nobody would believe me."

"What the hell are you talking about?"

"It'd be fake with me. With her, it's… right."

"Now you're an expert on Irish dancing."

"No. Just… Irish women."

"Let's get the hell out of this hellhole," he said, nonplussed, as he stormed out of the hotel, out of Ballymalloy, out of the running for the *Jazz* show and, if he but knew it, out of his dominance of his flashy but more perceptive partner. Mitzi didn't follow him but found her way to the office where Mary was still sitting on the edge of the couch, stroking Joy's hair, while Curly stood in the background, giving her room. Mitzi took in the situation immediately. She sat beside Mary and put her arm around her.

"I hear she was a dancer."

"Yes," said Mary, turning in surprise.

"Well, she would have been proud of you. And that Irish thing you did. Brilliant."

Mary looked at this flashy showgirl and saw only a sympathetic woman.

"Thank you."

"I'm sorry about that dangerous move that Darcy did."

"If it had happened you would have been hurt too."

"That's Darcy for you. He never sees the consequences of what he does."

"Must make life hard for you."

"Yeah. But interesting. Goodbye." She kissed Mary briefly and left. Mary and Curly exchanged glances. At that moment, two ambulancemen came in with a stretcher and moved towards the bed.

"Excuse me," said one. "We have to take the lady to the hospital. Do either of you want to come?"

"I'll come," said Father O'Grady.

"So will I," said Mary. She looked at Curly who shook his head and made for the door. The ambulancemen started to prepare Joy to be lifted onto the stretcher.

"Don't leave without me," said Mary as she followed Curly.

On the way out, they were confronted by Brother Nestor coming in, from whom the fumes of whisky wafted like mayflies on a still pool. He was not wearing his dog collar, but the tip of it could be seen sticking out of a side pocket.

"Brother business took longer than expected," said Nestor.

But they both ignored him. Outside in the street, Curly took the keys of the Buick from Artie, who waved a handful of banknotes at him.

"Thanks for these, Curly. I got 20 to 1 on you."

"Only a pleasure to pay you back, Artie."

Artie mumbled a 'congratulations' at Mary and passed on into the hotel to relieve himself of some of his well-gotten gains. She barely acknowledged it and moved to Curly.

"Where are you going to go now?" she asked.

"Another town."

"And another woman?"

Curly had the grace to be silent as he got into the car.

"Joy was a… great woman," he finally said.

"Yes. She liked you. Very much."

"I wonder why."

"I don't. I'll never forget you." She kissed her fingers and moved them across his lips.

"I wonder if I'll ever see you again," she said.

"You won't. But I'll see you. On stage in Dublin."

He started the car and drove away down the street. At the end of the hotel frontage, he stopped the Buick and threw the passenger door open. Mary took a half step towards it but stopped as Johnny burst out of the shadows carrying his trombone. He got into the car which drove away.

"Someone else to mentor, Curly Collins," she said as she turned back to the hotel and the waiting ambulance.

20

Picking up the pieces

Nestor collected his boys and shepherded them into the bus. His inebriated counting of the boys before leaving was interrupted by the remaining boys who were delighted at Johnny's escape and kept milling around while he tried to identify them and answered *anseo* (present) when he called out Johnny's name from the list. When he delivered the remaining boys back to the reformatory, he suffered no more than a mild rebuke from the Brother Superior who was rather relieved at having one boy less to take 'care' of. Johnny's name was removed from the files and it was as if he had never existed. The rest of the boys clung to the taste of freedom they had experienced in Ballymalloy and the glimpse they had had of a normal existence which to them seemed as the Paradise which the Brothers were forever dangling before them or even threatening them with. They shared these feelings – mostly of unbearable loss – when safe from the ever-prying, ever-suspicious eyes and ears of the ubiquitous Brothers. They also burned the sheets of jazz music with bursting hearts which, had they but known it, were as sore as those who had watched the burning of the great library of Alexandria.

Artie soon spent his considerable winnings and was relieved

when they were gone; they had caused so much profligacy in a naturally abstemious man and, at the same time, so much miserliness in a generous soul that he relapsed into gentle penury with secret relief.

Father O'Grady and his housekeeper took special care of Smack, who was manifestly sad at Joy's absence but soon recovered and was once again whizzing around town on his delivery bike, now sporting an exact replica of the mascot he had created for the Buick. Strangely, he never said 'Don't smack' again.

Ballymalloy took a while to recover from its moment in the sun. The dancers and the crowd disappeared. Those who had been poised to make a killing out of the contest were sadly disappointed. Those who had expected to make a little extra income did so. Very few denizens bothered to go to Dublin to see the *Jazz* show, or expressed any interest in it. St Patrick's Reformatory in Cork carried on as usual; starving, beating, exploiting, sexually abusing and sometimes killing its charges with impunity, as did the Mother and Baby homes and the nun-operated laundries with their bone-breaking chastisements, their psychological terror tactics and their blindness to the priests and bishops who used the girls in the most degrading way.

So, the festering sore of 'holy' Ireland carried on suppurating for the lifetimes – and beyond – of most of the unfortunate victims. Freddie held on to the hotel and, as Ireland slowly opened up to tourism, made a success of it and retired a relatively wealthy bachelor, a most respectable state for a man. Mrs Smith died in mid-quarrel and Mr Smith soon followed her, some said out of boredom.

Mary was chosen for the *Jazz* show, which was very successful in Dublin and travelled to the major cities in England and Western Europe. She developed into a skilled professional dancer but always sought ways of returning to traditional Irish dancing via the various competitions and dance festivals. Kilorglin became her chosen home and she looked after her Uncle Matt, who remained hale and hearty and light of foot for many years before passing gently away in his sleep one night, whereupon Mary married the proprietor of Kilorglin's most popular pub and bore him two children in prompt succession.

Curly's and Johnny's lives were on the border of professional performance and busking at the *feis ceols* and other festivals throughout Ireland. Johnny became a very competent jazzman, moving through a succession of bands and generally making a good life for himself. He cast off the horrors of his youth and delighted in the occasional busking tours of Ireland, with Curly dancing and him playing the trombone and fiddle, which he mastered very quickly. He envied Curly his casual but successful way with women and was happy to run away with him in the Buick from the occasional scandal. Curly's collection of jazz records wore out from so much playing and the frequent lifting off and dropping on the stylus. The Buick slowly disintegrated and lost its lovely well-rounded presence.

The gunsight mascot was never replaced.

Music URLs

CHAPTER 1

Peanut Vendor
https://www.youtube.com/watch?v=e_kIggnBnvk

Didn't He Ramble
https://www.youtube.com/watch?v=yt_pOf1QHDY

My Daddy Rocks M with one Steady Roll
https://www.youtube.com/watch?v=nzVCFiyCsoc

CHAPTER 2

Down by the Glenside
https://www.youtube.com/watch?v=Y_CrGMu83aw&start_
    radio=1&list=RDY_CrGMu83aw#t=23

CHAPTER 6

I Can't Get Started.
https://bunnyberiganmrtrumpet.com/2017/05/08/i-cant-get-
    started-1937/

Sean O Duibhir a Ghlanna
https://www.youtube.com/watch?v=GYfalhs5VC4

CHAPTER 7

Abdul a Bulbul Ameer
https://www.bing.com/videos/h?q=percy+french+songs&view=
    detail&mid=4ADF6071649ABA21284E4ADF6071649ABA2
    1284E&FORM=VIRE

American Patrol
https://www.youtube.com/watch?v=DK-lBi5r6Jk

CHAPTER 8

Sing Sing Sing
https://www.youtube.com/watch?v=GwPvLMlGWPI

CHAPTER 9

Moonlight Serenade
https://www.youtube.com/watch?v=8TB_8H23EDI

CHAPTER 10

In the Mood
https://www.youtube.com/watch?v=6vOUYry_5Nw

CHAPTER 11

Believe me if all those endearing young charms
https://www.youtube.com/watch?v=KF1e59-gX2I

CHAPTER 14

Peanut Vendor
https://www.youtube.com/watch?v=e_kIggnBnvk

CHAPTER 15

Skyliner
https://www.youtube.com/watch?v=lsDXnYKkdqw

Drowsie Maggie
https://www.youtube.com/watch?v=WIHI49JQ7zY

CHAPTER 16

Running Wild
https://www.youtube.com/watch?v=zBs9gZQX7lQ

The Foggy Dew
https://www.youtube.com/watch?v=NMOUCpoLB_8

CHAPTER 17

The Woodchopper's Ball
https://www.youtube.com/watch?v=6PcvT15IJ3g